OPERATOR B

EDWARD LEE

For Doug Clegg

PROLOGUE

"Dad? Mom?"

Stu and Sarah Billings simultaneously leaned up in bed; Sarah dragged the sheets up over her bosom, flicked on the lamp. *How's that for timing?* Stu thought, flushed in embarrassment. He'd been out of town on business for two weeks, and this was the first time since then that he and Sarah had a chance to…

In the bedroom doorway stood their thirteen-year-old daughter, Melissa, tall and slim in her flannel nightgown. She was rubbing sleep from her eyes but also… quivering.

"Honey, what's wrong?" her mother asked.

"You have a bad dream?" Stu guessed.

Their daughter just stood there for a few more seconds. When she lowered her fists from her eyes, it was obvious she'd been crying.

"I-I woke up," she peeped, "and…"

"What, honey?" Sarah asked.

"There was a man looking in my window."

Stu got up, hauled on his robe, then guided Melissa to the bed. "You stay here with your mother, honey. I'll go check it out."

"But Stu," Sarah fretted, "shouldn't we call the police?"

1

Stu considered this, then tossed a shoulder. "Naw, it's probably just one of those kids from down the road. They're always cutting through our yard at night to drink beer behind the fence."

Melissa sat next to her mother on the bed. "But Dad, this wasn't a kid. It was a man. He was bald."

"A lot of those punks shave their heads, honey. It's this Goth thing. Just stay here with Mom, and I'll be right back," Stu assured. "I promise."

Sarah hugged Melissa. "Your father's right, sweetheart. Everything will be all right..."

Yeah, Stu thought. When neither Sarah nor Melissa were looking, he quickly slipped the Smith & Wesson revolver out of the dresser and stuck it under his robe.

First, to Melissa's room. He peered out the window, saw nothing outside but the night. *Yeah, it's probably those pinhead punks. They drop out of school, shave their heads and put all these metal studs and rivets in their faces...and throw their empty beer cans in my yard.*

Of course, Melissa had probably just had a dream; she'd *dreamed* of the face in the window. The counselor at school had told Sarah and him it was typical.

Melissa had been only three years old when her father had been killed in a plane crash; her mother killed herself a year later. That's when Stu and Sarah had adopted her—immotile sperm had prevented them from having a child themselves. It didn't matter to Stu, nor to Sarah. They wanted a child and they got one.

And after ten years, neither of them even gave it thought that Melissa was adopted.

She was a model child. Intelligent, courteous, perseverant. A straight-A student at Sligo Junior High.

But she was shy, too. Pensive. Too often, she seemed bottled up, uncomfortable about revealing her feelings. The counselor had told them that even though she didn't *consciously* remember her early childhood and biological parents, there would indeed be some *sub*conscious shadows. Ghosts of things that weren't right, that weren't the way they were supposed to be. Melissa felt haunted but by what she didn't know.

Father dead, mother dead. Her whole world turned inside-out, Stu considered.

Didn't matter that she'd only been three. *Of course that's gonna have an impact on a kid, whatever the age.*

Stu walked down the long hall to the living room, then turned toward the kitchen and laundry room. This was the first time he regretted buying a one-level rancher. *That's just great, I've got these bald-headed Goth kids looking into my daughter's window. Christ...*

No one could be in the house; the ABC alarm would've gone off. In the laundry room, he stepped into his floppy yard boots, which he donned every Saturday to mow the grass. He turned off the alarm on the console by the door.

Then he went outside.

It was warm. Crickets trilled, making the air thrum. The darkness looked infinite. *Goth kids, huh?* he thought. *They think it's funny to scare my kid?*

He pulled out the Smith revolver, a .44.

We'll see who scares who.

He backtracked the opposite direction. If there really was a peeping tom, this would be his probable direction of escape. Stu's unlaced, booted feet took him around the back yard, across the patio, and then along the west side of the house.

He honestly expected to find nothing. What he found instead—

"Oh, shit!"

—was a tall, bald-headed man standing beside the azalea bushes.

"Calm down," the man said in the softest tone.

"The *fuck!*" Stu yelled, and all at once the sensation shocked him: snakes churning in his stomach. He jammed the gun forward. "You were staring into my daughter's window!"

"Yes, I was," the man said.

"You're a goddamn pervert! You get off looking at kids!"

"It's not that at all, nothing like that at all," the bald man said.

"Oh, it isn't?"

A stare-down in the warm noisy night. Mosquitoes buzzed about Stu's head. He pointed the revolver out straight, its sights lined directly onto the bald man's night-shadowed face.

"Let me give you some sound advice," the man offered. His voice flowed like some smooth liquid. "Never point a deadly weapon at someone you aren't fully prepared to kill."

The man held his hands half-up. Stu was sweating but maintaining his bead.

Then—

swish

The man's hands moved in a blur, snapped the revolver out of Stu's grasp.

Fuck, Stu thought.

"It's nothing like you think," the man said.

"I've got money, I've got two cars, credit cards, some jewelry," Stu said. "I'll give you whatever you want."

"To spare your life?"

"No, to spare my daughter and my wife."

4

The man wasn't pointing the gun back at Stu, he was just holding it. "And if I say that's not good enough?"

Fuck, Stu thought again. "Then I'll…fight you."

"Oh, a tough guy, huh?"

"I'm no tough guy," Stu said. "Christ, you just took a gun out of my hands in less time than it takes me to blink. But let's be real. I'll give you everything I have to leave my family alone. But the only way you're walking into my house is over my dead body." He didn't know where these words were coming from. In his terror he could barely think, and he was so scared he'd already pissed himself. "You got the gun. But if you miss, I'll gouge your eyes out, I'll bite your face off. I'll do *anything* to defend my family."

"Right answer," the man said. "Relax. Civilians don't handle stress very well." He handed the big pistol back to Stu.

What the—

"My name is Willard Farrington," the man said.

Wait a minute, Stu thought. *Farringt—*

"That's right," the man added. "I'm

Melissa's real father. That's the reason I was looking in her window. I just wanted to see her."

"But—"

"There's no time for that," the man said. "No time for explanations." He passed Stu a pale-blue piece of paper. "That's a routing number and an account index. I've deposited $500,000 in a trust for Melissa. You can't ever touch it. She can't touch it until she's eighteen. I can only hope that, as her father, you'll guide her to do the right thing with it. It's for her future, college, things like that."

Stu stared at the sheet. *Her father*, he thought. "They said you were killed in a—"

"There's no time for that," the man repeated. Then he looked at his watch. "They're on their way. I can't be here when

5

they arrive." Then the man tossed Stu what looked to be a shoebox. "This is for you and your wife, to help out. Don't be assholes with it. Take care of Melissa."

Stu, now in total disbelief, opened the top of the box. It was stuffed with bands of $100 bills. *This must be a couple hundred grand*, Stu realized.

"I—wait," Stu said.

"No time," the man said again. He lifted up the cuff of his left pant leg. A metal band lay atop his ankle. "It's a direction-finder. I've got to get out of here." The bald man stared at him amid the cricket cheeps. "You're a good man, I can tell."

Stu stared back.

"Take care of my daughter," the man said. "And don't ever tell her about this."

The pistol felt like dead weight in Stu's hand. Crooked under his elbow was the box of money.

A reef of clouds drifted away from the moon. Suddenly white light filled the yard, spilling onto the intruder's form. Stu noted the tears streaming down the strange man's face. He also noticed—

Mittens? Stu thought.

The man seemed to be wearing mittens. *Mittens, in summer?* But that was it.

Stu couldn't think of anything to say as the bald man disappeared across the yard into the darkness.

CHAPTER 1

From above the headboard, as if accusingly, the stiff faces stared down at him. Johann Steinhoff, Manfred Freiherr Von Richthofen, E.V. Rickenbacker, Adolf Galland.

The best pilots in history... And I'm probably better than any of them ever were.

General Willard Farrington lay back in the large, silk-draped bed. He hated the bed, by the way. He preferred a barracks rack any day of the week. Farrington was fifty-one years old now—when you got older, you were supposed to want nice things. But this place?

It was a palace. It could be likened to the Presidential Suite at the Mayflower Hotel. Genuine oil paintings hung on gilt-and-columbine-papered walls. Plush burnt-ocher carpets padded every footfall. Fine furniture, a twenty-four-hour attendant, even a hot tub, which he never used.

Recompense for his duty, his sacrifice.

But in all, the luxuriant suite proved little more than a well-appointed prison. His brief "escape" a week ago was something the mission staff should've anticipated...but what were they going to do? Fire him?

Farrington chuckled under his breath.

Oh, he understood the necessity of the quartering rules. *I'm special*, he thought. *I'm a living secret. I can never be seen.*

7

And he still, essentially, believed that.

He'd merely taken his unauthorized stroll because he needed to know that his daughter would be well-cared for. He needed to see her, this gift of his own creation that he'd willingly abandoned a decade ago for his duty.

Farrington still understood the duty. He just wasn't quite sure if he measured up any more.

I don't know if I can do it, he thought. Not this time.

Maybe he was burned out...

Duty, it was all about duty, wasn't it? The sacrifices of the few for the many. That's why he kept those sterile portraits hanging above his four-poster bed. In the many moments of doubt, all he need do was look up into these faces of greatness and see himself. But the reassurance was dwindling of late. *I've done my duty, haven't I?* he thought. *Why can't I just have a life?*

There's no going back, the portraits seemed to say. Don't forsake your honor. Steinhoff sneered at him, Rickenbacker bristled. *I've got more aerial combat kills than any of you fuckers,* Farrington thought, *but since most of mine are classified, I'll never be in the history books.* It wasn't fair. But Farrington, even in this rare moment of pouting pride, realized how wrong he was.

Certainly, the men above his headboard would all have sold their souls to have Farrington's privilege.

Stop being such a baby. Do your goddamn duty...

He lay back, his hands propped behind his head in the soft, goose-down pillow. He wondered what the woman thought when she first saw him. A hardcore military type? A busted old man? At least he kept in shape. The women were all wonderful actors. They acted like nothing was wrong when they saw his...

From the marbled bathroom, he heard the *hiss* of the shower creak off. At the same time, though, the intercom on the nightstand beeped.

"Sir, this is the CQ. Is everything all right?"

"Yes, Sergeant," Farrington answered. "Everything's terrific."

"Your dinner will be ready in—"

"Cancel it. I'm not hungry."

"Sir, you haven't eaten all day. I really think—"

"Cancel it," Farrington repeated with more edge in his voice. "And I don't want to be bothered for the rest of the night. That's an order."

A long hesitation. "Yes, sir."

The intercom clicked off.

Steam gusted like smoke when the bathroom door opened. The young woman sauntered out on beautiful long legs, all curves, flawless white skin, and green eyes like emerald fire. She was still trying, he had to give her that. But sometimes even men had "headaches."

She stood fully naked, unabashed, drying herself with the terry towel. "Some men like to watch, they like to look," she said.

Ain't working tonight, baby. "You're very beautiful," he admitted. But then so was his wife, who'd swallowed a bottle of insecticide a year after his "death" had been relayed to her. If that wasn't love, what was?

The woman propped one foot up on the bed, slowly drew the towel down her thigh and calf. "Hmm?"

Farrington knew the score. The Air Force contracted these girls all the time—the ones who weren't drug addicts or street scum—and paid them to "surrogate" special personnel. Sex ops, they were called; this *whore* probably had a Secret clearance. They mainly catered to the sexual whims of double agents in hiding, or demanding defectors.

And then there's me, he thought. *The one man the Air Force wants to keep happier than anyone else.*

He watched the sway of her perfect breasts as she continued with the towel. A quick glimpse at the soft thatch of her pubis nearly had him going. But he was tired of using people, just as he was often so tired of being used. That, or: *Maybe I'm just getting old.*

"Take your pants off," she whispered through the most sultry of grins. "I'll get you in the mood."

"No, really. Too much on my mind, you know?"

She stood straight, dumbfounded. "Well...this is the first time I've ever taken a shower in a client's place *before* I got dirty."

"I thought you'd like the digs," Farrington jested. "How many bathrooms you seen with genuine marble tile and gold fixtures?"

"Not many," she said. Clearly, though, she was insulted. She began to put her clothes back on right in front of him, her lips pursed.

Why should he care? Nevertheless, Farrington got up, walked to the silver cart and poured her a glass of Epernon from the obsidian black bottle in ice. "They always bring me these fancy wines when I have, uh, guests," he said and passed her the glass.

She stared at his hands for a moment, then took it.

"Aren't you having any?"

"No," he said. "I don't drink. I quit drinking in 1975 when Giap took Saigon. By then, I'd drunk enough Ba M'Ba to fill a gas station."

"God, this is wonderful," she commented, sipping. Then she picked up the bottle. "Jesus, this was bottled in 1914!"

"You like it?"

"Well, yes, but—"

Farrington stuffed the cork back in it, put it in a bag. "Take it. Show off to your friends."

"Well...thanks." She was dumbfounded—by the entire night. Farrington guessed the barrack chiefs had already paid her a thousand dollars for this. It was only money.

"But I'm sorry, you know," he said, "about the rest. Thanks for stopping by."

The woman looked confused through tousles of wet chestnut hair. "They paid me to stay till morning."

"Well then tonight's your lucky night. You're off early."

She blinked, incomprehension in the slits of her eyes. "Is there something—"

"Nothing wrong with you at all," he said. "I guess I'm having my period tonight."

She spared a laugh.

"The CQ will have a driver take you home," Farrington said.

She shrugged. "It's your dime."

Not really, it's the taxpayers'. "I'm glad you like the wine. But let me ask you something." Farrington's jaw set. He looked at her, then held up his strangely mittened hands. "Aren't you going to ask about...this?"

"They told me not to ask anything."

"Of course." What was he thinking? "Good night...and take care of yourself."

He showed her out, locked the ornate double doors behind her. *That's right, honey. Tonight's your lucky night...and tomorrow's my lucky day.*

He was staring into the mirror over a Hepplewhite dresser. An image flashed, and he saw himself a decade younger: firing up the grill on the patio of his Oxen Hill home. His smiling wife bringing out a bowl of potato salad to the picnic table. His perfect little daughter playing in the sandbox.

Then the image dissolved into the chisel-faced secret staring back at him.

11

The strange black mittens touched the dresser's brass knobs. He slid open the drawer, releasing a cedary scent of old wood. The framed picture of his wife remained facedown, as it always would. He couldn't look at it, but he couldn't throw it away either. Beside it, though, face up, lay a photograph from the '70s: Farrington, a major, standing in his Marine Corp flight suit on the ladder ramp of his Harrier V8B. He was surprised they'd let him keep it; any photograph of him was classified now.

His *face* was classified. All files of his existence had been officially deleted.

I'm deleted, he thought.

"Esprit d'corp," he whispered to himself. "Ain't duty grand?"

He stared at the drawer's remaining contents—trinkets. A Purple Heart, three Silver Stars, a Distinguished Service Cross, a Congressional Medal of Honor that Jimmy Carter had draped around his neck.

Only one more thing remained in the drawer...

———————————

The compound loomed behind her, a quiet fortress in plumes of sodium light. She kept the bottle of wine tucked under her arm, her high heels ticking across cement as she approached the lit gatehouse.

Her name was Tina, not that names mattered. She'd joined the Army in 1993 at age eighteen, hoping to escape a drunk mother and abusive father. When she'd passed the polygraphs—*Have you ever taken drugs? Do you gamble? Have you ever committed an act of theft?*—INSCOM had plucked her out of Basic and launched her career as a restricted sexual surrogate. A whore by any other name. She didn't care. She liked sex, and the money was good.

"Hello," she said. She held up the bottle of wine. "He said I could have this."

The young Air Force driver nodded at the gate. "One moment, please, ma'am," and he took the bottle into the gatehouse where an SP in a white helmet inspected it. A drab-blue government van sat just past the gatehouse, a door open. The van had no windows in the back, a protocol Tina was used to. She wasn't allowed to know where she was.

"Ma'am?"

Warm air swept past Tina's face. Her gaze drifted back to the strange compound. "This is one off-the-wall place," she commented. Then she remembered her "client's" hands. Once she serviced a Russian demolition expert who'd defected with blueprints for a SAGGER IV firing-trigger. His hands had been all but blown away. She wondered how he jerked off.

Tina knew she'd receive no answer but she asked the driver anyway, "What's wrong with that guy? He get burned or something?"

The driver stonily returned her bottle of wine. "Ma'am, I'm not authorized to disclose any information about your client, even if I was apprised of any such information, which I am not."

Tina almost laughed. These guys were all stock-in-trade, military automatons. *I'll bet he fucks like he's doing push-ups for a PT test...*

But a final thought slipped back to the nameless man whose suite she'd just left, the easiest trick of her life.

"He seems so sad," she said. "He seems afraid of something, terrified but trying to cover it up."

The driver did not respond. He showed her into the van and closed the door and moments later was driving away from this secret place back to the world of normal people.

Yes, one more object remained in the dresser drawer. Not a medal, not a commendation or combat pin.

Just a gun. Just an old Colt .45.

General Farrington stared into the mirror for the rest of the night, peering more at his life than his reflection. He saw it all, all that he'd been and all that he'd become.

Was it worth it?

Then he raised his black-mittened hands. He drew open each zipper in grueling slowness.

Was duty really worth this?

Every night now for nearly a month he'd put the pistol to his head, determined to end it all. And every night, he lost his nerve.

How would he fare tonight?

Unzipped now, he let the leather mittens fall to the floor. He raised his hands to the mirror in front of his face. The hands—

The hands deformed into things that no longer even appeared human. The hands laced with hundreds of intricate surgical scars and shiny with healed scar tissue.

Each of Farrington's hands possessed only two fingers and a thumb.

Monster hands.

He stared at them, and at his face beyond…

"Semper Fi," he whispered to himself. "Ooo-rah."

Then he picked up the gun.

CHAPTER 2

"Romeo One, this is Scratch One. Do you read?"
"Five by five, Scratch One. Go ahead."
"Request permission to land by vectored thrust option."
"Roger, Scratch One. Land your victor by vectored thrust on designated flight line and coordinates."

The plane dipped out of the sky, plummeting. Six hundred knots dropped to zero in 15.4 seconds. The engines groaned—not a promising sound—as the plane hovered as if levitating, then began to lower elegantly to the aluminum-treated asphalt.

When Colonel Jack Wentz landed the YF-61 on Runway 4 of Andrew's Tango-Delta site, he fully expected to die. It was a mind-set, it was necessary. The VDU and temp gauges read normal—nevertheless, he expected to die. In fact, of the thousands of times he'd landed planes during his career, he expected to die every time.

That way, he reasoned, if he *did* die, he wouldn't be surprised.

The wheel springs grated when he set down, then Wentz commenced with the proper system shut-downs. The Lockheed YF-61, though highly experimental (its turbines ran on hydrogen rather than conventional JP-6) looked just like an F-5E. Hence, there was no need to fly it at a black site.

Colonel Wentz was sick to death of black test sites.

The turbines wound down; Wentz popped the plex canopy and waited for Tech Sergeant Cole to wheel up the ladder.

How do you like that? Wentz said to himself. *I didn't die today.*

And he only had three more days to go.

"How's she handle, sir?" Cole asked when he hopped off the ladder.

Wentz passed him his CVC helmet and mask. "Like a barge. D-O-D wants to buy two hundred and fifty of these boat anchors at sixty-five million a pop? Shit. For a while I thought I was driving a five-ton Army truck over cinder blocks."

Cole edged close, whispering. "Come on, sir. What did she clock out at?"

"That's classified, Cole. You know better than to ask something like that." Wentz zipped down his collar. "But let me ask you something. In baseball, you get three strikes…and *how* many balls?"

Cole looked briefly puzzled. "Four, but—" Then his eyes shot wide. "You hit *mach f—*"

"Shut up, Cole. I thought we were talking about baseball." Wentz winked at his line attendant. "Now put my shit away and get me some coffee."

A squadron of F-16s roared overhead, drowning out Cole's laughter. Up in the flight tower, the duty controller flipped Wentz a thumbs up. Wentz waved back to the guy, knowing he'd never see him again.

"Look, Colonel," Cole said. "I know you're getting out on Monday. I just wanted to say it's been an honor to be your LA for these past couple of weeks."

"Don't get misty on me, Cole, I forgot my hanky." Wentz shook the man's hand. "And call me Jack. You're the best LA I've had in twenty-five years, so thanks. I'm throwing a retirement bash at my wife's place Monday night. If you don't show up, I'll have you transferred to chow-hall duty in Turkey as my last official act as an Air Force officer."

"I'll be there. Oh, and Top wants to see you in A Wing. ASAP."

Wentz snapped his gaze. "Gimme a break. I just unassed that flying coffin after five straight hours on stick. What's Top want?

Cole smiled knowingly. "Wouldn't know."

Wentz cast a suspicious eye. "It ain't cool to lie to full colonels, kid. Majors, warrant officers, first lueys—that's fine. But *not* full colonels. So what's going on?"

"Wouldn't know, Jack. Why don't you go find out?"

"Yeah." Wentz walked off the line toward the Dress Unit, sputtering under his breath.

Now in fatigues, Colonel Wentz approached the door which read A-WING F.O.D. 1ST SGT. CAUDILL. But everyone here called him "Top," as in Top Sergeant. Big, burly, and with a low southern drawl, Top was the highest-ranking enlisted man on the base. During Desert Storm, Top had hustled his 250-pound carcass around like a high-school kid, and ran an attack wing that launched over a hundred sorties a day without losing a bird. That's where he and Wentz had met.

"How's things in the land of coffee and donuts?" Wentz asked.

"Not bad," Top replied from behind an immaculate desk. "At least I can eat before I come to work and not worry about blowing chunks when I pull a 6-G."

"Top, there's only one thing you pull around here, and that's my chain. The kid on the line says you need to see me ASAP, so I'm wondering what the hell can Top possibly want to see me about when he knows I'm out of here on Monday?"

Top shrugged, took a sugary french cruller out of a Mr. Donut box. "I just wanted to know how the YF-61 flew."

"It's spam in a can. If the Air Force wants to put kids in those things, they better clock 'em five hundred hours of training time first. Otherwise, there's gonna be a whole lot of tax dollars sitting in the desert along with a whole bunch of kids."

"I watched you land her. Looked smooth to me," Top remarked.

"That's only because I'm the best pilot in the goddamn Air Force—"

"The most modest too—"

"And what's this all about anyway? You didn't call me in here to ask me about that hunk of junk."

Top's smile drew his jowls up. He slipped a piece of paper off his desk. "Got some orders for ya, Jack."

Wentz was instantly outraged. This was like a slap in the face. "I'm short and the CO is cutting me *orders*? Hey, he can send me to Alaska, but three days from now I'll be signing my retirement papers and turning in this monkey suit for good! I got eighty grand a year waiting for me flying 737s for United!"

Top closed his eyes, rubbed his temples. "I can't believe a hardcore Air Force driver like you wants to run off to fly those civvie air yachts. Look at all the cool stuff you get to fly for Uncle Sam."

"*Shit* on Uncle Sam. That old cracker's had me bent over his desk for twenty-five years, and he's never even kissed me. And you want to talk about the 'cool stuff' I get to fly? Cool, yeah." Wentz groaned. "Stuff that would make the Wright Brothers puke. I'm telling you, Top, I'm out of here in three days, and I don't care *where* those orders send me. If *God Himself* cut those orders, I'll kick His ass up and down Heaven Street. I'll slam St. Peter's Gate on His head and bust Him one in the nuts."

Top winced. "Relax, Jack. They're *promotion* orders."

The office fell silent along with Wentz's protests. His face felt a yard long staring at Top. "Guess what?" the First Sergeant continued. "You just made the big one star. Does that mean you're gonna start bossing me around now? I'm gonna have to start calling you sir?"

Wentz stood speechless.

Top got up from behind the desk and opened a small felt box containing two silver collar stars.

The stars glinted like jewels.

"Don't just stand there looking like you locked your keys in your car. Try 'em on…"

Wentz gazed longingly at the pair of stars, still unable to give voice.

"Here, allow me," Top said. He carefully pinned the stars onto Wentz's fatigue collar, then snapped to attention and saluted.

"Congratulations…*General* Wentz."

Wentz, still in a fog, turned to a mirror on the wall. General, the word slipped through his mind. The stars glittered back at him in the reflection.

"Hard-*fuckin'*-core, man," Top approved. "You're a *brigadier general* now, Jack. That's serious rank. And you know something else? You're a first."

"I'm a…*what*?" Jack asked, distracted.

"First time in the history of the United States Air Force they gave a general's star to a guy who's not an asshole!" Top blared. Then he yanked open his snack fridge, pulled out a bottle of Perier-Jouet champagne, and popped the cork. Foam poured on the floor.

"Shit, Top, thanks—"

Top poured the expensive bubbling wine into a pair of glasses, then passed one to Wentz.

"A toast. Here's to General Wentz…"

Wentz sipped from his glass. "General Wentz," he muttered. "You know, Top? I kind of like the sound of that."

The limousine idled at the gate, Department of the Air Force flags waving at its front fenders. Two Marine Corp MPs emerged before red signs in white letters that read:

PENTAGON WEST ENTRANCE.
THIS IS A CONTROLLED ACCESS. DUTY GUARDS HAVE THE RIGHT TO DETAIN ALL ADMITTEES REGARDLESS OF RANK OR OFFICE. YOU MAY BE ASKED TO BE SEARCHED.
THANK YOU FOR YOUR COMPLIANCE.

The first MP opened the limo door, while the second opened the phone box in the guard shack. General Gerald Cawthorne Rainier got out of the vehicle and dully returned the MP's crisp salute.

"Good afternoon, sir!" the MP barked.

"This may not be a very good afternoon at all, Sergeant," Rainier mouthed.

"Yes, sir!"

The line of four stars barely fit on the epaulets of Rainier's dress uniform. He was fifty-seven years old but right now he felt a hundred. No, this was not a good afternoon at all, not after the call he'd just received from SECPERS.

There might not be any good afternoons ever again, he thought.

His eyes lanced into the MP's gaze. "Tell security to have Briefing Room One prepped and swept ASAP. And open this goddamn gate."

"Yes, sir!"

Operator B

The MP shot a nod at the gate guard. The electric bolt snapped open, then Rainier brushed past, rushing into the west entrance as if trying to evade an augury of doom.

CHAPTER 3

In spite of the certainty of his retirement, Wentz felt funny in civilian clothes. He always had, as though high-alt flight suits had become as much a part of him as his skin. He felt funny driving cars, too, cautious to the point of paranoia—like a senior citizen behind the wheel. He remembered when he'd made the initial test flights of the B-2 bomber at Edward's Palmdale range, how natural it had felt on the stick of a prototype aircraft that cost nearly a billion dollars. But, somehow, driving a $20,000 station wagon felt daunting.

One thing that *did* feel right today, though, was the fact that his fourteen-year-old son, Pete, sat right next to him. Things would be different now. Now Wentz would actually get to be a father to his son. Today, they were on their way to Camden Yards, Yankees versus the Orioles.

"I couldn't do math either, Pete," Wentz was saying. "I hated it—algebra, trig, geometry. But I worked my tail off, hung in there, and made it. You've got to get those math grades up— C's won't cut it. Not if you want to get into a good—"

"I aced the final, Dad," Pete told him. "I got a ninety-nine."

Wentz was taken aback. "You're kidding me? A *ninety-nine?*"

Shit, I never got a ninety-nine on an algebra test in my life!

"Yeah, so I'll get a B for the course. A's in everything else."

Wentz slapped the wheel. *That's my boy!* "Hey, that's great, Pete! Now you'll make the honor roll! Outstanding! Buddy, we are *celebrating* this weekend! The Yankees game tonight, King's Dominion tomorrow, crabbing on the bay all day Sunday, and…you know what? I think maybe we'll do a little dirt-bike shopping once school lets out for the summer. How's that sound?"

"Thanks, Dad," Pete said. But it was a glum response, despondent. The boy seemed miles away.

Wentz glanced over. "Hey, partner, what's wrong? You look like somebody shot your dog…and you don't even *have* a dog."

"Well…Mom said…"

Wentz smirked. "What? What did your mother say?"

"She said you might be bluffing."

"Bluffing about what?"

Pete shrugged morosely. "About retiring from the Air Force."

Damn it! Wentz ground his teeth, then pulled the station wagon over to the shoulder and skidded to a stop. He looked right at his son. "Pete, when I told you and Mom that I'm leaving the Air Force, I meant it."

"Really?"

"Really, Pete. Look, I know it's been tough on you and your mother. Half the time I wasn't around—no wonder she divorced me. But we've been talking about it for months, and it's settled. On Monday I retire, your mother and I get back together, and we'll be a family again."

"Yeah, but you said that a bunch of times in the past, and then it never happened."

Shit, Wentz thought. Nothing he could say could make it right. Even the truth was an excuse. "Yeah, but that's because stuff came up at the last minute that I had to do for the Air Force. You know, stuff I'm not allowed to talk about."

"Secret stuff."

"Yeah. That's why I was never around very much. I *had* to do it, Pete. When you're in the service you have to obey orders."

"I know."

When Wentz glimpsed his own face in the windshield's reflection, the basest impulse urged him to punch it, to just put his fist right through the safety glass. In one second he saw all of his regret—and all of his arrogance disguised as service. *This is my son, for Christ's sake, and I'm snow-jobbing him. I'm making excuses.* When Pete was four, he'd almost died from pneumonia; Wentz was flying a classified recon op over North Korea. When Pete had hit his first home run in Little League, Wentz was flying at 100,000 feet testing new fuel-tank seals in an SR-71. And when Pete had been sent home from school for fighting, when he'd most needed a father's counsel and discipline, Wentz had been joyriding a YF-22 Advanced Tactical Fighter over the White Sides Mountain Test Reservation.

Some fucking father, he thought. *Always passing the buck to Joyce, always too busy playing Big Bad Top Secret Flyboy.*

"I'm telling you, Pete, that stuff in the past—it changes now. Your mother's giving me one more shot, and it's no jive this time. We're patching things up, getting back together, and it's going to work out."

For the first time since he'd gotten in the car, Pete looked genuinely enthused.

"And you'll move back to the house?"

"No, I'm going to pitch a tent in the back yard. *Of course* I'm moving back to the house! I've got my stuff all packed, got the mover lined up. It's a done deal."

Pete's eyes widened on Wentz. "You promise?"

"Roger that, buddy-bro," Wentz said with no hesitation. "You can count on it." He pulled the car back onto the road. "And there's nothing in the world that'll make me break that promise. Now let's go watch the Yankees kick some tail."

The office stood dark. Beneath a wan lamp, the folder lay open on the desk.

The leader sheet on the right read:

TOP SECRET
EYES ONLY - RESTRICTED:

OFFICER   EVALUATION   REPORT   (OER)
DEPARTMENT   OF   THE   NAVY,   MARINE   CORP
BRANCH.

Subject: FARRINGTON, WILLARD, E.
Grade: 0-7/DOB 13 FEB 48. SERVICE
#220-76-1455
Spouse: (DECEASED)
Children: ONE (F/ADOPTED)
Other Living Relatives: NONE

DE: DETACHMENT 4,
UNITED STATES AIR FORCE
AERIAL INTELLIGENCE COMMAND
FORT BELVOIR, VIRGINIA.

DUPLICATION OF THE ENCLOSED IS PUNISHABLE
BY DEATH VIA AIR FORCE REGULATION 200-2 AND
U.S.C. 797 OF THE INTERNAL SECURITY ACT.

TOP SECRET

A personnel photograph was fastened to the left side of the folder, and staring up from its glossy surface was the face of General Willard Farrington.

A hand closed the folder. A sputter was heard. Bold typeface on the folder's manila cover read:

OPERATOR "A"

It was General Rainier's hand which closed the MILPERS folder, and it was his voice which muttered, "God *damn*," a moment later.

Another officer—a major—sat in the room, submerged in darkness. He was a Tekna/Byman liaison field agent; hence his name was classified.

"Jesus," Rainier said. "Who would've thought something like this would happen?"

"It all went so well for so long, sir," the Major responded. "Perhaps we took the circumstances for granted."

Rainier looked up testily. "Yeah, I guess we did. The guy's been doing it for more than ten years without a hitch."

"Yes, sir, but remember the retrieval timetable. We don't have another ten years. We don't even have ten months."

"And you're telling me there's no alternate?"

A slight crack in the Major's voice betrayed his nervousness. "N-no, sir. Given the highly critical criterion, not to mention the most recent Presidential amendments to AR200-2, it was deemed too sensitive a risk to have a fully briefed and fully trained alternate on line."

Rainier strummed his fingers on the desk. "I've never heard anything so reckless and ill-advised in my life. Matters like this should never be disclosed to these ludicrous temporary occupants of the White House."

"You can be sure, though, sir, that the President *hasn't* been briefed on the QSR4 data."

26

"Thank God."

It was just a figure of speech, of course. General Rainier didn't actually believe in God. From where he sat, the lone desk lamp projected the shadow of Rainier's head onto the wall. It looked like a halo, and here was Rainier, the angel with no God. Instead his shrine was the Pentagon, and his church the most restricted warrens of the NSA. Technology—and death—were the only gods he could trust. He was probably the most powerful man in the United States' military, but it was all unofficial: an angel of might but with no wings. Only the jaded halo.

"And we do have a contingency, sir," the Major added as if to offer some consolation. "No one prepared, but at least—"

"You have someone in mind is what you're saying."

"Affirmative, sir."

The chair creaked when Rainier leaned back. He spoke with his eyes closed, struggling against a headache. "He's the best we've got?"

The Major stepped forward into the smudge of light and picked up the MILPERS folder labeled **OPERATOR "A"**. He inserted it into the feed slot of a Gressen automatic paper-pulverizer.

"He is now, sir."

The machine whined for a split instant, then disgorged its powder into a burn bag.

Presto—gone, Rainier thought. He wondered how many real lives he'd disposed of just as efficiently.

Next, the Major set down a second folder, this one labeled:

OPERATOR "B"

General Rainier opened the folder to glance down at a personnel photo of a lean-faced, hard-eyed white male in his forties.

"The candidate's name is Jack Wentz," the Major augmented. "He was promoted to general O-7 two days ago. He's been Top Secret/SI with eleven suffixes for more than twenty years, and he's our senior restricted test pilot. He's also got more black flying hours than any man in the world."

Rainier appraised the face in the photo as if calculating an ancient arcana. His fingers continued to strum the desk, and he wondered how angels felt when they struck down innocents with their swords in the name of God.

"Get him," Rainier said.

CHAPTER 4

Something scrabbled in the box, a chittering noise. There was something alive inside.

"Careful," Wentz warned. "Once they grab you, they don't let go."

Pete stared fascinated into the Styrofoam box. "I didn't even know they got this big, Dad."

Wentz pulled the station wagon into the driveway. "See, Pete, your old man's not as dumb as he looks. I know a guy in the Coast Guard who had to chart part of the Chesapeake for the government a few years ago, and they have this thing called thermal sonar. That's why we went to the West River estuary, 'cos this friend of mine, see, his sonar picked up thousands of really big crabs out there. No one knows about the place except me and him."

"Cool," Pete enthused. "Thermal sonar."

"Come on. Your mother'll never believe it."

Wentz grabbed the crab traps while Pete brought the box. Wentz felt strange walking up the driveway of the quaint Alexandria colonial, a house he'd bought a decade ago and had soon thereafter moved out of when Joyce divorced him for familial negligence. Wentz deserved it, of course. He'd promised her three times he was retiring—then canceled his retirement papers. He'd scheduled vacations with her and Pete, then simply didn't show up. The last straw had been the time he'd promised her he was getting Christmas week off on leave time, then turned around to volunteer for special duty when he'd heard Test Command was looking for sign-ups for a variable-wing mini-fighter.

What a tube steak I was, he thought now, lugging the gear into the garage. War was one thing, but joyriding was no reason to snow-job your family. In truth, Wentz didn't want some other stick-jockey to fly something that he hadn't. He'd been jealous, so he'd abandoned his family.

Yeah, what a dick…

The out-processing counselor had made some pertinent points. Coming off twenty-five years of military service might mean some serious adjustments. And Wentz knew that he'd have to put any former bitterness aside or this simply wouldn't work. It was *Joyce* who'd agreed to give him this last chance. The rest lay with Wentz. *First thing on the To-Do List is stop being an asshole,* he thought.

That's why he hadn't said anything to her on Friday when he and Pete got home from the baseball game. He was pissed off royally when he'd learned that Joyce had told Pete he was bluffing about his retirement. But then he remembered what the counselor had said, about compromise, about making an effort to see the past from *Joyce's* viewpoint. *What right do I have to be pissed off about anything? he realized. She's the one giving me the chance. What did I ever do except let her down for ten years? Nothin'.*

So he'd said nothing about it.

"Damn it, Pete," Wentz said. "What's all this garbage in the garage? You know, you could do a better job keeping this place clean."

Pete looked dumbfounded at his father. "What? I cleaned it last week. There's nothing wrong—"

"Don't talk back to your father, son." Wentz pointed. "Like that tarp over there. Looks like you just threw a tarp over a pile of garbage. What's under there?"

"I don't know!" Pete exclaimed at the accusation.

"What's under there? You hiding something?"

Exasperated, Pete pulled up the tarp.

"Oh, wow, Dad! Thanks!"

Propped up on its kickstand was a brand-new Honda XR800 dirt bike.

"It's the latest model," Wentz said, "and wider tires for better traction. Ninety horsepower; you'll definitely be kicking up some dust. Just remember, you can't drive it on the road."

"Thanks, Dad!" Pete rejoiced, hugging his father. "You're great! Can we take it out now?"

"Let's do the crabs first. Then we'll take it out to Merkle's Farm."

Pete was ecstatic. But it wasn't just that Wentz had bought his son something he wanted; Wentz looked forward to showing Pete how to maintain the bike, how to heed the safety precautions, how to assume the responsibility of owning it.

Father stuff.

"Mom!" Pete shouted when they stomped into the kitchen. "Dad got me that Honda dirt bike! It's the best one they make!"

Joyce Wentz half-smiled, leaning against the counter. Statuesque, long chestnut hair and noon-blue eyes. "I hope he got you a helmet to go with it."

"Of course I did," Wentz assured. "And knee and elbow pads. I also told him he could pull wheelies in the back yard. That's okay with you, right, honey?"

"Funny guy."

Wentz kissed his wife on the cheek.

"Oh—jeeze," Joyce blurted. "No offense, but you guys smell like low tide and—"

31

"Cat food, right, Mom?" Pete answered.

Joyce paused through a queer expression. "Well, yeah—"

Wentz slapped his son on the back. "Like I was telling you, Pete. Your old man's not as dumb as he looks. It's a little trick I picked up when I did TDY at Whidbey Island. Puncture a can of cat food with an ice-pick and put it in the trap. On the west coast, the watermen all use cat food as crab bait instead of chicken necks."

"Well," Joyce remarked, "I guess cat food smells better than chicken necks... So just how many crabs *did* you catch? Last time you guys went out, you brought home two crabs."

"Check it out."

Wentz smiled when Pete opened up the styrofoam box. Joyce nearly shrieked when she looked inside.

"They're *huge*," she commented.

"Half a bushel," Wentz added. "We'd have caught more but we didn't have a bigger box."

"I have to admit, I'm impressed," Joyce said.

"You'll be even more impressed when we're cracking these suckers open," Wentz guaranteed. "Pete, put an inch of water in the pot and pour in a cup of vinegar. Then lay in the steamer tray."

"Okay, Dad."

Joyce curled her finger at Wentz. "We'll be right back, Pete."

She took Wentz by the hand into the dining room. Wentz paused to look at her, and thought, *Jesus, what a beautiful woman. What did I do to get this lucky?*

Last night, they'd made love for the first time in a year. It was wonderful... probably more for Wentz than for her; he hadn't exactly been the Man of the Hour, more like the Man of the Minute. They'd fallen asleep wrapped up in each other; Wentz slept dreamlessly. The only dream he wanted was in his arms.

He was about to kiss her, tell her he loved her, when she pressed a hand against his chest. Suddenly, she didn't look pleased.

"So what's with this dirt bike?" she sternly asked.

Wentz stood duped. "It's something he wanted so I bought it for him. What's the big deal?"

"The big deal is you can't *buy* your son."

Wentz's gazed thinned. "I'm not trying to *buy* him. He worked hard and got his math grades up, so I gave him a dirt bike. What, a father can't give his kid a present?"

"Not an *absentee* father," Joyce countered.

Careful, Jack warned himself. *Look at it from her side.* "The absentee part ends on Monday when I retire."

"Don't you get it? Giving your son presents whenever you decide to come around isn't *being* a father."

Bust my chops a little more, why don't you? But, still, Wentz remained silent, like a scolded child.

"It gives him the wrong impression about things, Jack."

"I thought he deserved it, that's all," Wentz said very slowly. "For getting a B in algebra."

"That's not how it works in a *family*. Don't you think you should've talked to me about it first?"

"Yes, you're right."

"Don't you think we should've given him the bike, Jack?"

"Yes, I'm sorry. I wasn't thinking."

Everything she said made sense, of course.

It always did. Wentz had no idea how to be a real father because he'd never been around to assume the role. He was just a guy who stopped by every now and then, bringing presents.

She faced him, her lips pursed, her arms crossed under her bosom. "If you really are going to make a go of this, Jack, you're going to have to do better than this."

As hard as Wentz wanted to keep it all in check...he couldn't. Suddenly he felt attacked, and the instinct to defend himself shattered his better judgment.

"Fine, great. I'm an asshole, I'm a prick. I'm an *absentee father* who buys his kid presents to cover up his guilt. But contrary to what you obviously believe, I really am going to try to make this work. It would really be nice if just once you could give me a break."

"I won't even respond to that," she said.

He couldn't help it now, he couldn't reel it back in. "And you know, it really *fucks* me up when you trash me to him."

"What are you talking about?"

Wentz nodded cockily. "The other day when we went to the baseball game, he asked me if I was *bluffing* about my retirement. He says you told him that."

Joyce's cold eyes didn't blink. "Considering your track record? What else am I supposed to think? And yesterday someone named First Sergeant Something-or-other called and said you were promoted to brigadier general."

Wentz stalled. "Oh, yeah, Top. They gave it to me after I made my last flight. I forgot to tell you because it honestly slipped my mind."

"You get promoted to *general* and it slips your mind?"

"It slipped my mind because it's not important to me. It's no big deal. It's just typical Air Force ploy; they give you a big promo as bait to get you to sign up for one more hitch."

Joyce smirked. "But *General* Wentz isn't taking the bait, huh?"

"No, General Wentz is not. And at noon tomorrow, General Wentz will be *retired*."

Her rancor seemed to drift off. "I just wish I could believe that. I believed it in the past and look what happened. How many times?"

Bottle it up! he commanded himself. *Keep your mouth shut!*

But he couldn't. The arrogant fighter-jock wouldn't allow it.

"Well, honey, I'm really sorry about that little thing we had called the Gulf War, and I'm really sorry about the classified orders I got reassigning me to Nellis and Tonopah, but there's not much you can do about it when you're on active duty."

"You could've gotten that waiver you were telling us about," Joyce reminded him.

"Certain kinds of classified orders prohibit early-out waivers—"

"It broke Pete's heart."

That's all she needed to say. It was like a guillotine falling. It ended the argument before it ever really got started. Wentz wanted to kick the wall, knock things over, bellow out loud, but then he realized why. Because he couldn't hack the truth; he was too selfish to admit it. Oh, yes, Joyce had every right to treat him like pond scum...because that's what he was until he proved otherwise.

And I will prove it, he swore to himself. *Damn it, I WILL.* He closed his eyes, took a deep breath, pushed his selfish angst aside.

He looked at Joyce.

"I'll make it up to you—" He raised a quick finger. "I know you've heard that one before, and I know I've let you and Pete down a bunch of times in the past. Just the fact that you're giving me one more chance makes me the luckiest man in the world. I won't screw it up this time—I swear to God. You gotta believe me."

"I know you mean it, Jack," she said, "but I also know you're a career pilot. You're *addicted* to flying; you all are—"

"No I'm not, for Christ's sake."

"Jack, I know a dozen other women whose husbands are all pilots—and they're all divorced, it's all the same."

Wentz nodded after thinking about it. "All right, I guess it is something like that, the adrenalin and all, the rush. When you get to fly the most sophisticated aircraft in the world, it does something to your ego, and, yeah, I guess I was addicted to the thrill. But that's behind me now."

"Is it really? You quit the Air Force tomorrow, and what happens next week? You start flying for the airlines. Right back in the saddle."

Was she right about this too? There was no time left to fool around. This truly was his last chance. "All right, you're justified in saying that. I'm just going from one plane to another. So—" Wentz walked to the walnut highboy where he kept his papers. He pulled open the top drawer, withdrew his employment contract with United Airlines, and ripped it up.

"I don't give a shit about that job," he asserted. "It's just busy work, and now that you mention it, it's gonna be pretty damn disappointing trading in a $50,000,000 mach-three-plus ATF for a jumbo jet that won't get out of its own way." Wentz balled up the shredded contract and tossed it in the trash.

"Do you really mean that?" she asked. "That's fine with me if you do. We don't need this big house. We can move someplace smaller, tighten the budget, get cheaper cars—"

"We don't have to do any of that," he told her. "I don't even *need* a job. When they promo'd me to brig general, my retirement pay went up about twenty percent. Plus...when you're a classified test pilot, you get this thing called SOM credit. It stands for special operating missions—it's a hazard pay bonus you get when you retire. Mine's been building up with interest for over twenty years."

Joyce peered at him.

"It's...a lot of money," Wentz admitted.

"So you're telling me you're never going to fly a plane again?"

"I'm not *telling* you, I'm *promising* you."

Her eyes looked as big as cue balls. "So…what will you do?"

"Give you a break, for one thing," he answered at once. "Drive Pete to and from school every day like you've been doing since kindergarten. I'll do stuff around the house, mow the lawn, weed the beds, shovel the driveway in the winter. I'll be a house husband—you think I give a shit? I look *good* in an apron. You've busted your tail for the last ten years, now I'll take up the slack. I'm not kidding about this, Joyce. You quit school to put me through college, now it's my turn. You can go back and get your degree. *I'll* wash the damn dishes. You can open a crafts store like you always wanted. It doesn't matter. Whatever you want, I'll do whatever it takes to see that you get it."

Joyce looked nearly shocked. "You're serious, aren't you?"

"Damn fuckin' straight."

"Don't cuss. Pete might hear you."

"Hey, Dad!" Pete called out from the kitchen. "The water's boiling!"

"I'll be right there," Wentz said. He put his arm around his wife, pulled her close. "You'll see," he whispered. "No more broken promises. And by the way…you're fuckin' beautiful."

Joyce blushed. "Don't cuss…"

He kissed her and went back into the kitchen.

"Yeah, that's boiling," Wentz observed of the pot. "Now I'll show you another of your old man's trick's." He opened the refrigerator, pulled out a large bottle of beer. "Once the water's boiling, you pour in about eight ounces of a good German marzen, or something with a lot of malt. It makes the crabmeat come out of the shell easier."

Pete watched as his father poured in some of the beer.

"What are you gonna do with the rest?" Joyce coyly asked.

"Drink it. What else? When you're in an SOM wing, you can't drink. They even polygraph you to make sure you're not lying. And since I'm not doing that stuff anymore…"

Wentz took a hit off the bottle.

"Wow. That's not bad," he said. "First beer I've had since Reagan was in office. A little Johnny Black would do well now…but I'm not complaining."

"The water's back to a boil," Pete alerted him.

"Better let me do that, Pete," Wentz said. "You grab 'em from the back, otherwise they'll tear your fingers up." One by one, then, he transferred the crabs from the box to the steamer. "Nothing personal, fellas," he said to the crabs. "But you'd do the same to me if you had the chance." Then he dumped in heaps of spices.

"How long does it take?" Pete asked.

"About thirty minutes, or when the trap doors come loose. Crabs this big might take a little longer."

"I can't wait!"

For the first time since he could remember, Joyce actually looked happy. *She believes me*, Wentz thought. It was a gratifying relief. They were a family again, through thick and thin. That's all Wentz wanted, more than anything.

And now it was looking like he'd get it.

"Get the mallets and placemats out, Pete," Wentz instructed. "And plenty of paper towels."

"Okay, Dad."

Wentz walked back over to Joyce, put his arm around her waist. *I'm not bullshitting this time*, he wanted to say, but what would be the point in that? He was determined to prove it.

I'll show her…

Several soft *thunks* seemed to resound from outside. Wentz wasn't even paying attention. But Pete heard it, and he looked out the kitchen window, pulling up the lace curtains.

"Hey, Dad. There's Air Force guys coming up the driveway."

The hell? Wentz went to the window, looked out. Sure enough, the first thing he noticed was the tell-tale powder-blue sedan parked at the curb. Two Air Force SP's remained stationed at the car, while one more approached the house.

"Who the hell are these fucking bohunkers?" Wentz said.

"Jack, don't cuss," Joyce implored.

Wentz loped to the foyer, then brusquely opened the front door after cne knock. "What do you want?"

A 1st lieutenant in summer dress stood curtly on the doorstep, built like a body builder. He wore a gunbelt and an armband which read AFSS - SP. "General Wentz?" he inquired.

"What do you want?" Wentz repeated.

"I'm Lieutenant Hamilton, Air Force Security Service Courier Detachment, and I have—"

"What do you want?" Wentz said as rudely as possible for the third time.

"I have an urgent hand-deliver-only TDY message, sir."

Wentz impatiently snatched the yellow piece of paper from Hamilton, then frowned when he read it.

"Who the hell's this?" he demanded. "What's he want to see me for?"

"It's classified, sir," Hamilton stated the obvious.

"Tell him I'm sick."

Hamilton just stared back, wooden-faced.

"Goddamn it! I'm cooking crabs with my kid!"

"Sir, it's an AFSS command order," Hamilton informed.

"I'm not coming, it's out of the question—"

Hamilton's brow rose. "Sir, if you don't come with us willingly…we have orders to—"

"*Damn* it!"

39

Wentz felt an inch tall when he turned around in the foyer. Joyce stood there looking back at him, glaring.

"I'm sorry, honey, but I gotta go to the base," Wentz said. "This muscle-rack and his goons will drag me there if I refuse."

She didn't say anything, but Wentz could read her lips when she said to herself: *Goddamn you…*

"I'm not bluffing about tomorrow, I swear. At one minute after noon, I'm a civilian. I give you my word."

"Just go," she said and walked up the stairs.

Pete looked in from the kitchen entrance, disappointment plain in his eyes.

Wentz held up his hands. "Pete, I'm sorry, man."

"It's all right, Dad. You gotta obey your orders."

"When the crabs are done, stick a few in the fridge for me."

"Okay, Dad."

Wentz seethed, humiliated. He glared at Hamilton, then looked up the stairwell.

"Joyce?"

No response.

"Joyce! Don't forget! Tomorrow, noon. Be there!"

Wentz turned and left the house. "You sons of bitches," he said right to Hamilton's face. "I ought to bust you down to E-1. I could, you know that?"

"I'm just doing my job, sir."

"Your job isn't to fuck up my life. I ought to transfer the lot of you to our tracking site in Nord, Alaska. See how you big bad SP's like some of that shit."

"We apologize for the inconvenience, sir."

My ass…

Guilt loomed behind Wentz like some huge, subcarnate shape as he walked down the driveway and got into the government sedan.

40

Operator B

When the sedan drove away, Wentz had no idea in the world that he would never see his wife and son again.

CHAPTER 5

Officially, Andrew's Air Force Base was not a test site. Officially, it functioned as the main transport hub for the Washington Military District and the President's primary personal airport.

*Un*officially, however, its northernmost perimeter was known (to those with the proper clearance) as Section Tango-Delta, a modest restricted test site. This had been Wentz's place of employment for the last month.

He had no time to change into his Class-A's, but that was fine with him and his current mood. He was about to meet the four-star general who'd destroyed his weekend less than twenty-four hours before his retirement.

Hence, Wentz found it appropriate to report in jeans, sneakers, and a New York Yankees t-shirt, smelling like cat food and bay water.

Hamilton and his AFSS apes escorted him to Section HQ, the CO's office.

Somehow Wentz wasn't surprised to see that the CO was not there.

Two Technical Services men were leaving just as Wentz was about to enter: Wentz was used to the sight. They'd swept the office for bugs and other potential live surveillance devices, magged the walls for passive mikes, and placed static grids over the windows to block a reflective-laser tap.

Tech Services, in other words, meant serious business. *This probably isn't a tea party*, Wentz reasoned.

The first thing Wentz saw when he entered were two rows of four stars. What he saw next was the tight, sallow face of a man nearing sixty, Westmoreland-ish, sharp-eyed in spite of the price of his years.

Wentz approached the desk, snapped to attention, and saluted. Less than enthusiastically, he said, "General Jack Wentz, B Scuadron, 41st Test Wing, reporting as ordered, sir."

His host sloppily returned the salute. "Drop the protocol, Wentz. I'm as sick of it as you are. Have a seat."

Wentz sat down, then craned his neck around. A captain with no name tag sat against the wall in a block of shadow. He looked like bad news. Beside him sat a female full colonel, a brunette, who appeared shockingly young. They both looked at Wentz with focused expressions.

"I'm General Rainier—" his host announced.

"Never heard of you, sir," Wentz said.

"—of the United States Air Force Aerial Intelligence Command."

Wentz repeated, "Never heard of it, sir."

"No one has," Rainier replied, "and we go to the utmost measures to keep it that way, Wentz. Now, I'll make this short. The woman to your left is Colonel Ashton. She works for me. The captain next to her, whose uniform obviously lacks a name tag—well, you know the drill."

"Great, a Tekna-Byman Op," Wentz recognized at once. The Air Force's version of Army CIC—their names were national security secrets. "Captain *Smith*, I presume?" Wentz posed.

"Captain Smith is fine, General," the man said.

"He has some questions for you," Rainier informed him.

"Smith" stood up, flipping through an aluminum-covered notebook like a traffic cop. Only this notebook had a lock on it.

"General Wentz, is it true that you led the initial F117 anti-fire-control raids—code-named Operation Slipcover—on 15 January, 1991?"

Wentz looked right back into Smith's face. "No."

"From May to December, 1993, did you test fly an experimental reconnaissance aircraft codenamed Aurora at the Tonopah Test Reservation in Nevada?"

"No," Wentz said.

"On 12 February, 1999, did you pilot a parachute mission which involved a low-altitude, low-opening air-drop of Army INSCOM field operatives over the province of Kosovo, twenty-four hours after which a brigade commander of Serbian security forces—a Colonel Zlav—was assassinated by long-range sniper fire?"

"No," Wentz said.

The room stood momentarily silent.

"All right, Wentz," Rainier played along. "Here's your passcard."

The General smiled sourly, then passed Wentz a 3x5 sealed plastic envelope that read:

RESTRICTED, EYES ONLY, WENTZ, J., USAF, 221-55-4668

Wentz broke off the perforated edge, then withdrew another plastic card that read:

4B6: VERBAL CLEARANCE.

Smith cleared his throat. "General? If you will?"

Wentz sighed. "Yeah, I led the Black Bird raids on the Iraqi HF radar sites twelve hours before the war started, and I did the same thing in Panama, and, yes, I LALO'd the INSCOM grunts that scratched that asshole in Kosovo. I flew the Aurora at Tonopah and the X-23 at Palmdale and the SCRAM-jets and nuclear ramjets at Holloman and Goodfellow. I've flown the YF-24, the F-22, the JSF, and the YF-118. When Lockheed got the bid for the B- 3, I was their flight-profile consultant. I've flown every classified aircraft we have, and I've participated in more classified aerial ops than I can remember, and with all due respect, sir—"

Rainier nodded. "We know, Wentz, you're retiring tomorrow. The thing is we have a problem, and you seem to be the only one qualified enough to resolve it."

Wentz scratched his chin. "Why me?"

The pretty colonel, Ashton, stood up from her chair. "Well, General, it comes on very good authority that you're the best pilot in the world."

"Are you?" Rainier asked.

Wentz didn't like this kind of spotlight. "I don't know. Maybe. I've probably got more black test flights than any one else. But there are plenty of guys out there who are top-notch."

"Top notch isn't good enough," Smith said.

Then Rainier: "If you're not the best, then who is?"

It didn't come easy, but Wentz put his ego aside. "Will Farrington," he admitted.

"You've flown with General Farrington?" Rainier asked.

"Well, no, sir. He was Marine Corp," Wentz said, "and what I heard was he retired as a colonel O-6."

Ashton again: "What do you know about Farrington?"

It was a difficult question to answer or to even contemplate. Like asking a World War I vet about Sergeant York or the French Foreign Legion in Indochina. Farrington was a myth, a legend within the secret circle of classified aviation. Any pilot who ever saw Farrington fly would never forget it. They said that on their deathbeds, the last thought in any woman's mind would be the first man she'd made love to.

With black-op pilots, the last thought in your head would be the time you saw Farrington fly...

"He was the best test in the business, bar none," Wentz said. "No one could touch him. When he grabbed the stick, he became part of the aircraft. In 1984 I saw him pull a barrel roll in a C-141. This guy could fly cargo planes like they were fighters, and he could pull Immelmann Turns in *helicopters*. In Vietnam he brought down sixteen MIGs in a Douglas Skyraider, guns only... There was a war correspondent in Hue who actually filmed Farrington in his Skyraider—a propeller-driven plane—shooting down four jet-powered MIGs like they were slow skeet—not with air-to-air missiles, with mounted guns. First day in test-pilot school, they show that film. Will Farrington was astounding. Kind of like everybody's icon, the pilot's pilot. He was the King Zeus of black-op flyers and restricted test pilots."

"What became of him?" inquired Smith. "Do you know? Did you ever hear any rumors?"

"He disappeared in '88," Wentz said. "Word is he retired and became a recluse; they said he burned out. Didn't make sense for a driver that good to retire."

"That's because he didn't *retire*, General," Smith informed. "He's been working for us since then, on a very classified project."

Wentz peered at Smith, then at Rainier. "You want me to work with Will Farrington?"

"Would that change your mind about retiring?" Rainier asked.

These goddamn people kill me, Wentz thought.

"No."

General Rainier and Smith traded narrow glances.

"That's not quite it," Rainier continued. "What we want, Wentz, is for you to pick up where Farrington left off."

Wentz didn't know if he felt more puzzled than pissed off. "I don't get it, sir."

General Rainier leaned back in his chair with a sigh. "Farrington committed suicide several nights ago. We was clinically depressed because—well, we think he lacked the confidence to undertake his current mission. We want *you* to consider that mission."

Wentz felt floored. Suddenly a whirlwind of questions rose, all bidden by his pilot's propensities and the instincts formed over the last twenty-five years of sitting in classified cockpits. What "mission" could possibly daunt a flyer the likes of Will Farrington? What mission would cause the best pilot in the world—and in aviation history—to *kill* himself?

Part of Wentz found the notion unfathomable...but it also hooked him.

If Farrington couldn't hack the mission...maybe I can, he tempted himself.

But then the reality swept back down, the promises he'd made, and not just those to Joyce and Pete but those to himself.

"I can't, sir," he said. "I can't do it."

"Scared? Ain't got the nuts?"

Wentz uttered the most irreducible chuckle. He knew what he wanted to say in response, thought about all the reasons why he *shouldn't*, but then said it anyway.

"Fuck yourself, sir."

Ashton and Smith went rigid.

Wentz tossed a shoulder. "That's right, I just told a four-star general to *fuck himself.*" He shot his gaze across the room. "You haul me away from my family with all this crypto spook show bullshit and have the audacity to insult me with mind-game challenges that wouldn't work on a high school kid?" Wentz

47

pointed at General Rainier. "If you think I'm scared, if you think I ain't got the nuts—try sitting in one of *my* chairs one motherfucking day, General. Try test-flying a plane with reverse-angle wings where even the goddamn designers don't know if it'll fly for more than fifteen seconds before falling apart. Try flying six hundred and fifty knots at an altitude of twenty feet in the dark, just to drop a single laze marker and knowing if you hit a tree or a powerline, a couple of hundred grunts are gonna die along with yourself. Try that, sir. You and your kind get carted around in an Air Force limo; you've probably got a master sergeant to hold your dick for you when you piss. Try pissing your pants in a ramjet when the systems light goes off, when you've got two choices, you can eject and drop your plane in a residential neighborhood and wipe out a block, or you can try to glide fifty miles to the water and flop a hundred million bucks in the drink when you know you've only got one chance in ten of surviving the impact. I did that once. So, I repeat, sir. Fuck yourself."

Wentz had expended his rant, and probably his honorable discharge. *Fuck it*, he thought.

Ashton, and Smith stood wide-eyed in shock. Rainier strummed his fingers on the desk.

"I don't like to be played with," Wentz said to the silent room. Then, to Rainier, "Go ahead and demote me to basic airman. See if I give a shit."

"This isn't about that," Rainier said, unperturbed. "This isn't about protocol or UCMJ or rank or who's the top cat. Christ, I wish more men had the balls to talk to me like you just did. The reason you're here isn't about any of that Air Force bullshit."

"What *is* it about then?"

"Total duty, total service to one's country."

Wentz ground his teeth until he could taste the metal in his fillings. "For twenty-five fuckin' years, I've served my country like a waiter, and I never even asked for a tip. Remember the Gulf War, the CNN shot of the Paveway II laser-guided bomb swerving into a single window on a sixteen-story office building? That was me. I took out Iraq's Office of Tactical Air Command, and after flying so low to make the hit, my plane got punched through by so much triple-A my wings were *whistling*. I couldn't even make it back to the base at Jiddah; I had to eject over the Gulf... Two hours after Air-Sea Rescue picked me up, I was flying another sortie. So don't tell me about duty. Don't tell me about service... Sir."

I would never presume to," Rainier's voice grated. "We know all about your feats. We know all about the many times you've risked your life for your country. And that's the reason you're here instead of some *other* cocky flyboy. You're the *best*. We need the *best*."

Smith stepped forward, holding classified evaluation reports. "Our performance indexes are processed through every personnel computer in the United States military, the CIA, and NASA. You were quite right. General Willard Farrington was the best pilot in the world. But now he's gone. Which means that *you* are now the best pilot in the world."

Shit, Wentz thought.

Rainier offered a minuscule smile, stroking his beardless chin. "It's unlike any mission you could ever imagine."

"I can't take it," Wentz insisted. "It doesn't matter. I'm retiring tomorrow. I promised my ex-wife and kid."

"Don't you at least want to know what the mission is?"

Wentz felt his fingernails scraping his palms. "No, because if you tell me, then I'll just be that much more tempted to take it."

Rainier eyed Smith and Ashton, cocked a brow. "A proposition, then. I *won't* tell you. Check it out for yourself."

"What do you mean, sir?" Wentz asked.

"Fly out to Nellis, right now, with Colonel Ashton. Assess the mission. If you don't want it, that's fine. We'll get someone else, and I give you my personal guarantee that you'll be back here tomorrow by noon to attend your retirement ceremony."

Wentz gnawed his lower lip. "Putting it that way makes it damn hard to pass up, sir."

"All we're asking is that you investigate the mission and its details first-hand, General," Smith stepped back in.

"And if I don't like it, I walk?"

"Absolutely, sir. We'll fly you straight back to this base and you can officially retire. Beyond that, the only thing we'd ask of you is perhaps a list of other qualified candidates, men you've personally known who you feel might be able to assume the mission's requirements."

Wentz's resolve began to bow, then it collapsed altogether. He rationalized, of course, manipulated the proposition around his promise like a sculptor covering up a flaw with a last-minute slap of clay.

He wasn't going to accept the mission…

I'm just going to check it out. What's the harm in that?

"All right," Wentz agreed.

"Outstanding," Rainier said. "Squared away."

Wentz came to attention, saluted but Rainier just waved a lazy hand. "I told you, forget about all that. If I have to return one more salute, my goddamn arm's going to fall off. Colonel Ashton?"

The woman moved forward, a perfumed shadow. "Get your flight gear on, General Wentz. There's an F-15 waiting for us on Taxiway Six. On afterburners, we should be in Nevada in about fifty minutes."

Operator B

Wentz scoffed. "With *me* flying? Try forty."

CHAPTER 6

Static crackled on the headset. "Romeo One this is Boxcars One. Request permission to…" Wentz paused. Why should he care about proper commo protocol anymore? "Request permission to open this fucker up to the max and get the fuck out of here."

A chuckle through the static. "Permission affirmed, Boxcars One. You are clear for take-off. When you melt the runway, we'll send you a bill."

"Good luck making me pay, Romeo One. Adios…"

Taking off on afterburners was close to impossible—but not for Wentz. You just had to know how to jink the throttle in tandem with the azimuth. The $40,000,000 plane didn't take off as much as it *exploded* off T-D Runway 4. Wentz wasn't fifty feet off the asphalt when he pulled into a full barrel-spin and was burning upward at nearly a forty-five-degree line. They were a corkscrew soaring straight up.

Wentz watched the heavens revolve in the polycarb canopy: the world was a bright spinning top. Ashton shrieked like a cat on fire.

"Stop it! Stop it! I'm going to—"

Wentz leveled off with a single quick jerk of the stick. In one second, the plane was flying flat and smooth, roaring westward, the sun beaming above the sky.

He could hear Ashton gasping in his commo set. "You okay, Colonel?"

A few more gasps, then the otherwise reserved Colonel Ashton shouted, "Look, I'm not into this fighter-jock macho crap, damn you! Fly the plane normal!"

"I thought that's what I was doing," Wentz miked back to her. "Tighten your stomach muscles. I'll show you normal." More finesse on the stick, and the plane's wings were perpendicular to the Earth as he pulled into a 4-G climb.

"Stop it! Stop it!" she shrieked. "Please!"

Guess it's time to stop being a dickhead, Wentz considered. He leveled off again. "I'm sorry, Colonel. I just thought you'd want to experience an official takeoff record. We just climbed to 58,000 feet in one minute. That's a record for this aircraft. Now you've got something to tell your grandkids."

Ashton sat behind Wentz, in what would otherwise be the Bear's Seat, or the EWO seat—electronic warfare officer. This F-15M2-series was a courier version: minimal AV bay, no ECM pod, no General Electric M61 gun. It was stripped, in other words, all business. Two seats sitting on top of two modified Pratt-Whitney dual-shaft turbofans rated 40,000 pounds of zero-mean thrust apiece. The fuel-burn-rating was classified, and so was the plane's top speed: mach three-point-one. The only thing that struck him as odd was the paint scheme: flat Khaki paint, solid, like the color of sand.

"I almost...*peed* myself!" Ashton shouted through her mike. "I don't care if you're the best pilot in the world! Don't do anymore of that shit!"

Wentz winced at the word. "Colonel? If I may make a personal observation? Somehow, hearing the word *shit* come out of your mouth...well, it doesn't become you."

"Fuck off!"

Neither does that, Wentz thought. "I apologize, Colonel. I'm just having a little last-minute fun. After tomorrow, I'll never be flying this fast again."

An exhalation over the wire somehow sounded coy. "Still don't think you'll take the mission?"

"Positive. Rainier was playing me for a fool, so I thought I'd return the favor. Thought I'd take the opportunity to drive an Eagle one more time, at his expense. Whatever this mission is, I ain't taking it."

The coyness left her voice. Now she sounded dead serious. "Don't be too sure."

Wentz cut his afterburners when the temp needle was about to max. "All right, let's forget about keeping a jackass in suspense. Tell me the mission."

"No way, sir. You need to see for yourself, just like General Rainier said."

"Eee-haw, eee-haw," Wentz said. "And by the way, what's with the funky paint on the plane?"

"You'll see."

Great answer. "Okay, but if you don't mind my asking, what's an... attractive... woman like you doing in all this super-secret classified security clearance bullshit?"

"You know something, General? Even Farrington wasn't as sexist as you."

"Sexist!" Wentz objected. "Where'd that come from?"

"Most of you guys? Jesus. Because you're so maladjusted and unsocialized, you pull these macho big-stud pilot antics. You think that turns a woman on. You think women melt when they see a hardline test pilot in uniform. Well, let me tell you something, General. I've met a lot of pilots in this business, and every single one of them has been an egotistical self-absorbed high-on-himself *asshole*."

54

Wentz chuckled. "Then I'm glad I haven't disappointed you, Colonel."

"Boxcars One, this is Romeo One. Do you read?"

"Roger," Wentz answered. "Is there a problem?"

"No problem, Boxcars One. We just wanted to let you know that our planar-array WLR confirms that you just set an official climb record for an aircraft of your designated thrust-rating."

"Roger, Romeo One. Tell me something I don't already know. Boxcars One, out." Wentz smiled. "See?" he miked back to Ashton. "I told you."

"I'm not terribly impressed, General," Ashton shot back. "And what's with the 'Boxcars?' Isn't that a symbol of ill omen?"

"Sure," Wentz said. "Every time I land a plane, I expect to die, and I always pick a callsign that's bad luck. Widow-maker, Plane Thirteen, Lockheed Casket Company, stuff like that. When I flew the Aurora, my call-sign was Dead Man One. It appeases the fates. It nullifies bad luck by giving reverence to it—it's pilot stuff. We call it The Nix. If you don't worship The Nix...you're spam in a can. There won't be enough left of you for an E-2 crash technician to scrape out of the cockpit with a spatula."

"The Nix, huh?"

"Yeah."

Another coy silence, then Ashton's voice lowered. "You might need a lot more than The Nix to save you now."

"Think so? We'll see. I already told you, I'm not taking the mission, whatever it is."

Silence.

Then, "Oh, you'll take it, General," Ashton said. "I guarantee you'll take it."

Wentz laughed out loud in his mask. "Keep dreaming, lady! I'm just here for the stick time..."

Fifteen minutes later, Wentz keyed his mike. "We're coming up."

"All right, General," Ashton replied. "Slight change of destination. We're not really going to Nellis."

"What? So where are we going? Tasty-Freeze?"

"Proceed past Nellis Main Runway 3 to Papoose Lake, seventy-five miles west, southwest."

Alarmed, Wentz jerked his head around to look at her. "Papoose Lake? That's a priority no-fly perimeter! I can't land there!"

Ashton passed forward another plastic envelope. Wentz tore it open and removed a card that read:

4B6: PILOT - (SI) TEKNA/BYMAN/ULTIMA - COMMAND ORDER – BYPASS AS INSTRUCTED.

Wentz just shook his head, adjusting the pitch-trim. "Whatever you say, lady." He kept one eye on the E-scope, then he veered the stick and peeled off toward the new coordinates. *The spook show continues*, he thought. Papoose was a lake that had dried up hundreds of years ago, and since Wentz's first day as a pilot, any aerial passage over the ten-thousand-acre perimeter was strictly prohibited by the FAA, the Bureau of Land Management, and U.S. Air Force Security Group Activity. No one knew why but it was easy to guess. A dried-up lake? Thousands of acres of desert? Irradiated waste disposal, or a chemical/biological dump, Wentz presumed.

Below him, the desert stretched endlessly, humped by ridges of sand dunes. "So where am I going to land?" he asked Ashton. "On the sand dunes?"

"There's a runway. You just can't see it."

"What?"

"Switch on your inertial-navigation director and turn your automatic blue-flight toggle to 'alt.' Set your heading to four-three-one, then activate auto-pilot."

Smirking, Wentz did as instructed.

"Now turn on your ECM jammer pod—"

"This is a courier! There's no ECM on this plane!" Wentz barked.

"No, but there's something else connected to its console."

Dismayed, Wentz flipped up the ENABLE switch. Suddenly the sky-toe display snapped on, and—

What the—

—the aircraft began to descend, pivot, and maneuver for landing, all without Wentz doing a thing. Of course, auto-landers existed but were rarely used, and even when they were, it was always necessary for the pilot to visually line up a computer mark with the landing zone.

But, here, there *was* no landing zone.

All Wentz could see below him were the endless hillocks of sand.

"It's some kind of a pulse-navaid, isn't it?" Wentz asked. "It receives emissions from a ground-based VOR and terrain-following radar, then feeds it all into an onboard processor, right?"

"Do you see any radar antennas or VOR dishes, General?"

Wentz strained his eyes. He saw nothing but sand.

"Besides," Ashton added over the commo line, "a half-hour from now, you're not even going to care."

"Still think I'm taking the mission, huh?"

"Yes, sir."

Her presumptuousness continued to amuse him to no end, but as the plane's altitude began to drop, Wentz's concern rose.

She'd said something about a runway that couldn't be seen. But where? The dunes?

"Where are we going anyway?"

"A base," Ashton answered.

Wentz stared down. Only sand dunes.

"I don't see any damn base—"

Then the landing gear began to lower on its own. The flaps dropped, and power began to retard.

"Relax, General," Ashton said.

Wentz was not relaxed. He began to fidget. After all these years, he'd forgotten how to be afraid.

But now he was remembering again.

When the altimeter read ninety feet, he did something he hadn't done in decades: he panicked.

"Something's wrong! The INS must've blown its boards!"

"Relax, General," Ashton calmly repeated.

"We can't land in sand! I'm going to punch us out—"

"Do NOT eject!" Ashton shouted. "The runway is camouflaged! Do NOT eject!"

Camou—Wentz grit his teeth, staring at the desertscape before him. The tires chirped when the plane touched down. Wentz expected the nose to pitch; he expected an explosion and summary death...

But the plane landed normally in what appeared to be...sand.

Smooth as silk, he thought. "What, the runway—"

"The runway is made of a sand-colored composite," Ashton said.

"Yeah, but...you can't see it."

"That's the idea."

Power dwindled to normal taxi speed.

"Disable your ECM switch and take over," Ashton instructed. "Taxi ahead at zero-forward degrees and keep your eyes peeled for the ground guide."

Wentz felt stupid, maladroit. Back at the controls, he peered ahead and eventually spotted a man in sand-colored fatigues beckoning them forward with his hands. "I can barely see the guy!"

"Yes, General, and now it's probably all starting to make some sense."

A completely subterranean air base? he wondered. *Impossible...*

The ground guide shoved out his palms—*Stop*—then made a cut-throat gesture. Wentz braked and shut down the engines.

"What happens now?" he complained to his passenger. "We go play in the dunes? Build a big sand castle?"

The ground began to shake beneath a deep sonorous hum. Wentz remained dumbfounded. Then the ground beneath them, in a long rectangle, began to *lower*.

A flight elevator, he realized. Like on a carrier, only this was in the desert, *part* of the desert.

"An underground site," he said over his mike.

"Yep. Impossible to detect. A lot of those sand dunes are hangar exits. The base has twelve aircraft lifts, all virtually invisible."

Wentz had seen a lot of military trickery in his time—rubber submarines in Groton, Connecticut; "pseudopod" LF radar generators that cost $100,000,000 per unit; an entire communications complex in Lincoln, Nebraska, whose sole purpose was to manufacture counterfeit radio traffic—but this took it all. The elevator platform lowered the plane some twenty feet, after which a taxi crew zipped forward from out of the dark. Within thirty seconds, a Cushman electric goat pulled the plane backward, then the elevator rose again and sealed shut. Immediately afterward, another crew of men drove mobile vacuums over the platform grid, sucking up sand.

"Now you see the reason for the khaki paint job?" Ashton asked.

But Wentz was rocked. He popped the canopy, gazing out in questioning belief...or disbelief.

An entire installation beneath the Earth. Wentz pulled off his flight helmet and air-mask, disconnected his CVC lines. Unconsciously, he unfastened his safety harness. His eyes felt sewn open as he looked around.

Hooded lights lit corridors of metal and cement which stretched further than he could see.

Droves of Air Force techs in white jumpsuits and white hardhats milled about like ants each with a separate duty.

"Fuckin'-A," Wentz muttered.

"Come on, General," Ashton prodded. Techs pushed a wheeled ladder to the cockpit. Wentz and Ashton climbed out and down.

"Group! Heads up!" one of the rankless techs shouted. "Officers on the floorwall!"

Another more authoritative voice bellowed, "Snap to, shit-heads! This ain't the fuckin' Army! This is the *Air Force*! I want you turds standing tall! Colonel Ashton's just brought a *general* in here. Show him how it's done!"

"Group Level One! Atteeeeeen*tion!*"

Heels snapped in a single echoic *CLAP!* when the droves of white-suited "ants" came to attention and offered perfect salutes. In similarly perfect unison they shouted, "Good afternoon, sir!"

"What is this, the boys' fucking choir!" the voice belted out. "This man's a hero! He's won medals! He's risked his life for us! He was taking enemy flak when you were all playing grab-ass

60

and jerking off in high school! You will show him respect! Now sound off like you're in the Air Force, not the National Guard!"

"GOOD AFTERNOON, SIR!"

The vocal report resounded like a cannon shot. Wentz tremored, lifted an inch off his heels. He just stared at them all with his jaw hanging.

"General?" Ashton reminded.

"Oh…yeah." He and Ashton returned the salutes.

Wentz, in a stunned moment, held the age-old military gesture. For as far as he could see, men in white jumpsuits stood straight as chess pieces, holding their salutes in dead silence.

"Sir?" Ashton whispered. "Drop your salute and offer a counter salutation." *Oh…yeah.* Wentz dropped his right hand and droned, "Uh, carry on men."

"You heard the General!" returned the bellow. "What the fuck is this, a Navy lunch break? You gonna eat quiche with a napkin in your laps? You gonna sip espresso and talk about art? Back to fuckin' work, ladies, or I'll send you all out into the fuckin' desert and the last trace of *all* your sorry asses will be little pieces of fingernails in buzzard shit!"

Jeeze, Wentz thought. *These guys are hardcore, they're worse than the Marines.* The men instantly returned to their nameless duties as a maintenance crew taxied the plane further away into a service cove.

Wentz's awe sat on his shoulder like a pet parrot as he followed Ashton down what appeared to be the main access passage for this veritable underground terminal. Luminous taxi lanes branched out from various angles, each ending at its own elevator platform.

"Where are the hangars?" Wentz asked. "Deeper, much deeper." Ashton's flight boots clicked on a floor that looked like seamless steel plate, painted glossy black. "Three of them, in fact, are six hundred feet deep, built into layered bunkers that will withstand a fifty-megaton subsurface detonation."

"This place must've cost billions."

"Nintey-five billion to be exact—"

Wentz gaped. "That almost one-third of the annual defense budget!"

"This is all black money, General. Uncle Sam has ways that would surprise you. The facility consumes nearly ten billion a year just in maintenance and operating costs. This is Level One, obviously the surface-access level—this is just the top of the cake."

"Experimental aircraft is what we're talking about here, right?"

"That's right. Things even you have never flown, sir. Mostly the newer variant EM-Crafts."

"EM-Crafts?" Wentz grew mildly jealous. He thought he'd flown it all. "What the hell is an EM—"

"Northrop makes them in Pennsylvania. You've heard of rail guns?"

"Sure, but its only theory."

Ashton smiled. "Don't believe everything you read in *Popular Science*, General. We have operational SDI rail guns in orbit right now."

"Isn't that, like, a horrendous violation of the latest ABM treaty?"

"Yep. Anyway, the EM-Craft is a rail gun in reverse. A graduated chain of electromagnetic-pulse energy provides thrust for the plane. Top speed is 7000 knots."

"Get out of here," Wentz said. "Even the Aurora doesn't go that fast."

Ashton smiled at his objection. "General, compared to the aircraft in this facility, the Aurora is a Sopwith Camel. We've got three different nuclear ramjets, none of which you've flown, we've got F-18s refit with liquid-oxygen-stream propulsion systems, and we've got a new wingless stealth fighter—"

"Not wingless," Wentz interrupted, "you mean a flying wing, like the B-2."

"I mean *wingless*, General. It's eleven meters long and looks like a black pencil. No wings, no tail, no flaps. It's a flying tube."

Wentz was getting ticked. "But that defies all the standard laws of aeronautics!"

"No, it doesn't," Ashton sniped back.

"Then how can it possibly maneuver in the air?"

"Vector vents in the rear, gyroscopes in the nose."

Wentz didn't believe it, but then what else *could* he believe when he looked around at this immense place? Suddenly, excitement pumped through him. EM-Crafts, new-series ramjets, wingless fighter prototypes?

"So *that's* what they want me for," Wentz presumed, following Ashton to what appeared to be the end of the terminal. "To fly this new stuff."

"Nope," Ashton said.

"What do you mean *nope*?" Wentz complained. Her response sounded like an insult. "That weirdo captain and crackpot old four-star back in Maryland just verified that I'm the best pilot in the damn world. Why can't *I* fly this stuff?"

"You're far too valuable," she oddly answered. "There are dozens of excellent pilots here. The Air Force would be crazy to let a man of your skill fly the planes we've got here."

"Why?" Wentz nearly whined.

"Too dangerous. The planes here are *highly* experimental. This facility averages ten pilot-deaths per year due to crashes. You only get to fly the planes that have been perfected and deemed safe. The Air Force has too much money and training time invested to let you die in a crash."

63

The comment disheartened him. "So the initial pilots are fodder...until the engineers can work out all the bugs."

"It sounds cold, but, yes. You don't want to know how many pilots died in Aurora prototypes before it could be improved enough to let you fly the first official test runs."

Wentz swallowed dryly. *I'm walking on men's graves. Every time I got behind a new stick...I was sitting in a ghost's seat...*

"I wouldn't dwell on it, sir," Ashton offered. "Like General Rainier said. It's all about service, it's all about duty. You were too valuable to the country to risk in a plane that hadn't been sufficiently tested. That's the bottom line."

"Yeah, well I don't *like* the bottom line. The bottom line eats sh—"

Two guards in unmarked black fatigues stood before a shiny personnel elevator, each brandishing M249 rifles with 200-round box drums. They eyed Wentz coldly, then parted when they noticed Ashton. A disturbing sign was mounted above the doors:

THIS ELEVATOR DE-POWERS AT DEFCON ONE. DO NOT USE IN THE EVENT OF FIRE OR IMMINENT NUCLEAR STRIKE.

The elevator opened only after both sentries simultaneously inserted code cards into slots and pressed their right index fingers on an optical pad.

"This joint is serious business," Wentz remarked once inside the elevator.

"Yes, it is."

"But how come the guards didn't ID me?"

"Because you're with me."

Wentz took the speculation further. "Well suppose I was holding you hostage, suppose I had dynamite under my flight suit and I'd ordered you to act normal or I'd set it off?"

"One of the screws in that warning sign was actually a digital lens connected to a cadmium thermograph. If it detected any heat fluctuations on my face—distress—an alarm would've sounded."

"What then?"

"The guards would've machine-gunned you without hesitation."

"Like I said," Wentz repeated with raised brows. "This joint is serious business." Then he noted no floor-indicator on the elevator, no floor buttons. "How do we know where we're going?"

"It's already been preprogrammed, but for your information, we're going to the facility's deepest level. I think you'll like it: Level Thirteen."

Wentz praised The Nix. "All right, Colonel, so what's the rest of the scoop? Papoose is a total fake? They always said it was a toxic waste dump or something."

"Yes, that's the cover story we planted years ago."

"I learn something new every day." He stole a glance at her; she looked puny in the flight suit, preposterously young. "Now tell me something else. How's a twenty-year-old manage to make full colonel?"

"Very funny, General. I'm twenty-nine, not that it's any of your business. I'm just an admin officer."

Wentz couldn't help the chuckle. "Right, just an admin officer...with instant access to a black test site and a security clearance higher than the Chairman of the Senate Intelligence Committee."

The elevator doors hissed open, leading them out into a white, antiseptic corridor. "Ready to find out why you're taking

65

the mission?" Ashton asked. She stopped next to a pair of white doors which read DRESSING UNITS - MALE - FEMALE.

"I'm not taking the mission," Wentz assured her. "But I sure as shit want to find out what it is."

"Then get into your fatigues and I'll show you." Ashton paused. "Oh, I almost forgot."

"What's that?" Wentz asked.

"Welcome to Area S-4, sir."

CHAPTER 7

Dressed in white fatigues, Wentz and Ashton stood in an empty darkened warehouse hundreds of feet long.

"Area S-4, huh?" Wentz commented. "What's it stand for?"

"Just a designation. It's actually a federal land grid. And there's no tagline for this facility—no Groom, no Dreamland, no Skunkworks."

Wentz looked down at his attire, frowning. "Well, so far I'm impressed, but I'm not exactly digging the white fatigues. Makes me feel like a house painter. And what are we just standing around for?"

"We're waiting for someone…"

Hard footsteps clapped in the distance, growing closer. *Who's this dweeb?* Wentz wondered. *He looks like Wally Cleaver.*

A young collegiate-looking officer eventually appeared, wearing an Air Force Class-A uniform and major's blossoms. No name plate.

"Great," Wentz said. "Another Tekna/Byman Op. Let me guess—Major *Jones*, right?"

The two men shook hands. "Jones is as good a name as any, General Wentz," the Major replied. "I'm honored to meet you, and I welcome you to Area S-4. If you'll follow me please, sir."

They began to cross the empty warehouse, their footsteps all clattering. But as Wentz squinted, he noted that the underground warehouse wasn't as empty as he'd thought. Along the far walls, hidden in shadow, stood armed black-garbed sentries every ten feet. Moments later, then, he noticed machine-gun emplacements built into the walls high above them. The barely visible gun barrels followed them as they proceeded.

That's some Welcome Wagon, Wentz thought. "Area S-4. And all this time I thought 51 in Tonopah was the blackest test site in the world."

"There's one blacker, General, and you're in it," Major "Jones" said. "I take it you've spent a lot of time at Area 51?"

"I practically lived there off and on for ten years. That damn sand-pit cost me my marriage."

Jones glanced to Ashton, then nodded.

"General, you're familiar with the cult UFO hype surrounding Area 51?" Ashton asked him.

Wentz smiled, bemused. "Sure. I read about it every time I'm in line at the grocery store. Dead alien bodies on ice. Crashed spaceships in secret hangars. The local residents have some sort of a club out there; they think the 0315 Black Goose flights are UFOs that we've captured."

"But what is *your* conclusion, General?" Jones queried.

What else could Wentz do but frown? "I've walked every square foot of every warehouse, hangar, and building at Area 51, and I've never seen any spaceships or dead aliens. Now would you *please* cut the jive and—"

Jones stopped, handing Wentz a metal clipboard. "I'm sure you're more than familiar with the National Classified Secrets Act, sir."

"The Federal Secrecy Oath is like death and taxes." Wentz didn't need to read it; he just signed it and passed it back to Jones. "I'll bet I've signed more of these than you've signed credit card receipts."

They walked a ways further, then came to a halt before a huge steel bulkhead painted white. Blue letters read:

DEADLY FORCE PERIMETER
UNAUTHORIZED PERSONNEL
WILL BE KILLED

That's putting it bluntly, Wentz thought.

Jones and Ashton exchanged odd glances, like an inside joke.

Wentz shot them both a hard look. "Wait a minute. Just wait. You're not gonna tell me that you've got dead aliens in there."

"No, General," Jones said.

He inserted a tubular key into a small plate. The immense steel door began to rise almost soundlessly.

Ashton tapped Wentz on the shoulder.

"We keep the dead aliens in Ohio, sir," she said.

Back in Maryland, General Gerald Cawthorne Rainier, as he was known to, strummed his fingers on the desk blotter. He chain-smoked, knowing it would kill him someday, and he often hoped that day might come sooner than later.

Often, he felt he deserved it.

The smoke swirled before the desk lamp, the only illumination in the office. Rainier preferred the dark. It seemed vastly easier—and much more appropriate—to sit in the dark when he contorted and manipulated the lives of good men.

He stared down at the open folder, stared down at the personnel photo of Jack Wentz. Then he closed it and stared at the heading:

OPERATOR "B"

He pushed it aside as the gauzy air swirled before the lamp. How many dead faces did he see in the smoke, how many ruined souls?

He forced himself not to consider the questions—he was good at that. His fingers continued to strum.

Next he placed a single sheet of thin tractor-fed paper on the desk blotter.

READ AND DESTROY

TOP SECRET
(SI/HS) BYMAN/BYMAN/FARGO

AF-MILNET CIPHER:

PAGE ONE OF ONE PAGE

CRYPTMAIL CODE 49867-99-00
-25 JULY 1999 -0713 HRS

FROM: NSA/DIRECTOR OF
ENCRYPTED OPERATIONS, FT.
MEADE, MARYLAND

DE: LEVEL THIRTEEN, AREA S-4,
TECHNICAL TESTING FACILITY,
STAPLES, NEVADA
DE: NASA, ANALYSIS BRANCH,
GREENBELT, MARYLAND

TO: IGA (INTER-AGENCY GROUP
ACTIVITY) THE PENTAGON

SPECULATION AND ASSESSMENT:
(CODENAME) QSR4

ELINT CONTROL BRANCH, CENTRAL
INTELLIGENCE, LANGLEY, VIRGINIA.

PLEASE ADVISE.

END AF-MILNET CIPHER

READ AND DESTROY

General Rainier leaned back in his chair and dropped the sheet into the automatic paper-pulverizer. The machine grated for a split second, then fell silent.

Rainier lit another cigarette, watched the smoke unfurl before the light like so many homeless spirits.

One day, he knew, his own face would be floating in the smoke.

As the heavy bulkhead door rose, so did a line of light across Wentz's face. When the door had lifted completely, a loud CLACK! was heard as steel pins locked it open.

No, he thought, peering ahead. *No. No. No. No. No.*

He was staring at what was clearly an air vehicle of some kind, but one with no configuration he could imagine as being capable of flight.

It was crescent-shaped, not circular or disk-like. Wentz imagined a giant heel. It was thirty feet long, twenty feet wide. Dull silver, like sandblasted aluminum.

No. No. No...

Armed guards walked a slow post around it, while still more guards looked down from gun emplacements high overhead in scaffolds. Floodlights beamed down, harsh as desert sun.

Wentz felt his astonishment sift away, replaced by something like numb shock. All the blood seemed to have drained from his face.

"No," he croaked. "No way."

"You know what this is, don't you, General Wentz?" Jones asked.

Wentz stood dumb and mute, staring.

"General?"

A team of technicians approached the vehicle, brandishing aerosol paint tanks on their backs. They began to paint the object, tan on the topside, sky-blue on the underside.

"The paint burns off almost immediately," Ashton remarked, "but it serves as sufficient camouflage during take-offs. The KH and RENSKY satellites can't see it. Then we wait until after dark to bring her back, with the same auto-landing hardware that was installed in the F-15."

"What's it called?" Wentz managed to ask.

"We call it the OEV," Jones replied.

Then Ashton defined, "Operational Extraterrestrial Vehicle."

My God, Wentz thought.

Jones went on to explain. "Since 1944, the military has documented over sixty instances of vehicles of extraterrestrial origin crashing within the continental United States. Most of these vehicles were completely destroyed upon impact. Four were recovered reasonably intact but rendered inoperable via crash damage... General Wentz? Are you listening?"

Wentz nodded slowly, his mouth open, his eyes flat.

"One vehicle, however, was recovered *completely* intact, and that would be the vehicle you're looking at. It was recovered outside of Edgewood, Maryland, in 1989. It is our estimation that the OEV didn't crash but instead landed near the U.S. Army's Edgewood Arsenal. The vehicle's two occupants then disembarked upon what we believe was a field survey of several weapons depots on the Edgewood installation, whereupon they were shot and killed by post sentries. In other words, General, the OEV is—"

"Undamaged," Wentz dully replied. "Still flies."

"That's correct, sir. It is fully operational as we speak... General? Are you *listening*?"

Wentz mutely nodded again. He could not divert his stare.

"Give him a break," Ashton said to Jones. "It takes time."

Jones seemed exasperated. "I know this is difficult, General, I know this comes as the biggest shock of your life. But you must listen carefully. Will Farrington was the OEV's primary operator."

"Will Farrington is dead," Wentz guttered.

"Yes, sir. And that means that you are now the vehicle's primary operator—"

Snap out of it! Wentz shouted at himself. *Jesus Christ, this is serious. You're looking at a fucking UFO! Snap out of it!* He broke from his paralyzed stance and quickly approached one of the guards.

"You," he ordered.

The guard snapped to attention. "Yes, sir! Good afternoon, sir!"

"Fuck that good afternoon shit. Slap me in the face. Hard."

The black-suited guard blinked. "Sir, I can't strike an—"

"Do it!"

The guard lowered his M-17 4.4mm ACR rifle and—

CRACK!

—slapped Wentz across the face so hard he saw stars. "As you were," he bumbled, shaking off the rest of his stupor. *Wow, that hurt.* He blinked out the bright spots, then paced briskly back to Jones and Ashton.

"All right," he said. "My shit's square and I'm good to go. Now...show me the inside of this bird."

———————————

They'd climbed aboard via a standard Air Force hull ladder. The OEV sported a circular hatch a yard wide, and next Wentz was stepping in, following Ashton down another ladder that clearly was not manufactured by the Air Force—the rungs and side-rails of *this* ladder were thin as wire but supported Wentz's weight without so much as bowing. Now Wentz stood at the bottom of a yard-wide tube, the same dull silver as the pre-painted hull. *An airlock,* he guessed. Red instructions had been stenciled:

CAUTION: SET DECOMPRESS (30-SECONDS EGRESSION TIME) ACTIVATE DETENT, THEN DEBARK

Wentz stepped through the airlock's oval man-way; Ashton stood waiting for him.

"Sweet Jesus," Wentz murmured when he glanced forward, starboard and port.

The interior stood stark, smoothly featured. There were no signs of original flight controls in the "cockpit," though several banks of indicators had been mounted by Air Force technicians, as were two high-tech flight chairs installed over two contoured humps that clearly were the pilot and co-pilot seats of the vehicle's original operators. Wentz leaned over and peered through two prism-shaped windows beyond which he could see the maintenance scaffolds and the interior hangar. The small windows bore no indication of casements, seams, frames, or sealant—as if they'd somehow been *grown* into the front of the craft. Aside from the sparse man-made additions, everything inside was the same color as the outside, that dull, lusterless silver.

"I don't know if I believe this," Wentz said.

"Once you fly it, you will."

He examined the aft section. Some supply compartments had been installed, a SNAP-4 nuclear battery and water cell, and an EVA rack, but he didn't notice anything that might resemble an engine compartment, nor fuel stores.

"What's the fuel source?" he asked the first logical question.

"Unknown. Our physicists believe it has something to do with gravity amplification synchronized with or against magnetic-pulse waves. We're confident that the manner in which the vehicle harnesses available energy is unlimited."

"Endless fuel source…"

"More than likely, yes," Ashton concurred. She pointed to a cylindrical object protruding on the floor, molded into the coaming. It was no bigger than a Coke can. "We believe *that* is the gravity amplifier, or what you would think of as an engine. More than likely, other navigational and guidance components exist in the hull. The crew were oxygen/nitrogen breathers just like us. It's more than likely that the air supply is also unlimited."

"That's a lot of 'more than likely's,'" Wentz posed. "I don't want to be the driver at the stick when this thing runs out of gas."

"I've been in it during many of Farrington's para-orbital flights. So if I'm not worried about it, a big tough senior test like you shouldn't be either."

Wentz didn't exactly appreciate Ashton's rising snippiness, but he hardly cared.

"Top speed?" he asked.

"Unknown. Within the Earth's atmosphere we estimate a maximum forward velocity of about 50,000 miles per hour."

"Impossible. The inertia would turn the pilot into ground chuck."

Ashton's slippy manner edged back. "General, this vehicle wasn't built by Boeing or McDonnell-Douglas; it was built by *alien* engineers. You're *standing* right in the middle of the proof. You have to modify your powers of belief. Once you get it in your head that this isn't a balsa-wood plane with rubber-band propeller, we'll all be better off."

"All right, Colonel Smart Ass," Wentz shot back. "Then you tell me how an aircraft can travel 50,000 knots and not smash the pilot's brain against the inside of his skull, pop his eyeballs, squirt his spinal fluid out his ears, and blow all of his internal organs out his mouth and his *asshole*?"

Ashton shrugged as if these considerations meant nothing. "General, we're obviously dealing with a technological base that's probably a thousand years ahead of us. It's only logical that the OEV is fitted with some sort of integrated hypersonic envelope that counters forward inertia with reverse inertia, precisely in time with acceleration. Who cares how it works? It just does."

"All right, fine. So how fast is it...*out* of the atmosphere?"

"Again, unknown. All we *do* know is that the propulsion system is capable of producing velocities that seem to be exponentially faster than—"

"No, no! Don't even say it!" Wentz nearly yelled.

"—the speed of light. Farrington's longest-range flight was to Alpha Centauri. It took him four days instead of four years."

Shit, he thought. How could he object?

"Let me put it this way, General. Everything you've ever believed before today...is wrong."

Frustrated, Wentz combed his gaze around the cockpit area. "Where are the controls? Where's the stick?"

76

"Keep cranking that rubber band, sir. There's no *stick*. This is a para-orbital, hypersonic, self-contained intragalactic transport unit. It's founded on technologies that are virtually unknown to the human race."

Wentz was getting pissed. "I don't care if it's a goddamn Good Humor truck! How do you fly it without controls?"

Ashton's tone moderated. "The controls are...integrated."

"Integrated with what?"

"With the operator—the pilot..."

Wentz squinted at her like a caveman glimpsing the ocean for the first time.

Ashton touched the brushed-silver surface of an angled ledge in front of the port-side flight chair.

A seamless panel *hummed* open.

"What in the holy hell?" Wentz asked.

The opened panel revealed two narrowly outlined indentations. Outlines like two bizarre hands possessing only two fingers and a thumb.

Ashton audibly gulped. "Those are the controls," she said.

CHAPTER 8

"Those things," Wentz said, "those outlines. They're handprints, aren't they?"

They'd left the hangar and now sat in a brightly lit in-briefing room, Jones behind a standard industrial-gray military desk, Wentz and Ashton in opposing armchairs.

"We don't call them handprints, General," Major Jones explained. "We call them operator detents."

Ashton, then: "Synaptic activity in the brain is processed into and out of the detents by way of the median and ulnar nerves in the arms and the collateral nerve branches in the fingers."

"You're talking about thought, aren't you?" Wentz figured. "I put my hands against those handprints, *think*, and the thing flies?"

Jones nodded yes. "That's correct, General. It seems that thought conduction on the part of the operator is effectively converted to operational commands which are processed into the vehicle's guidance system."

"Fly-by-wire, only the pilot's *nerves* are the wires..."

"Precisely," said Ashton.

"And, hopefully, General, given what you've witnessed today, you'll be canceling your retirement plans."

Wentz closed his eyes and heard a deafening silence. Behind the lids, he saw an insuperable void, a vastness like looking down from the highest places on the Earth. He saw a pilot's most fantastic dream come true, and then he saw the faces of Joyce and Pete…

"I can't," he said. "I promised my wife and kid. I've been breaking promises to them for the last ten years, but I can't *break* this one."

A final tempt, a final image to maraud his pilot's ego: he saw somebody else, some other pilot bestowed with this impossible honor. *It'd be some punk,* he guessed, *probably some boner'd up hot shot Navy kid from Whidbey NSA or Miramar or, worse, a Blue Angel. Am I really gonna step down and let some cocky F-18 PUNK fill my shoes?*

"Shit! GodDAMN!" Wentz bellowed.

Ashton and Jones just looked at him.

"Ain't happening," Wentz said through a painful grimace. Part of him could not conceive of what he was about to say. "I'm not going to fuck my family over again. Tomorrow at noon I retire. Get someone else."

Jones leaned forward, amazed. "Are you serious?"

"Right now, I'm so pissed off I could kick you in the balls so hard they'd fly out your mouth. Does that sound serious? Do you have any idea how hard this is for me?"

"General, don't you realize what we've got here?" Jones induced. "The OEV isn't some—"

"Yeah, yeah, I know, it's not some balsawood plane with a rubber-band prop. I already got that shtick from her. I know what it is, but I also know I can't do it."

Jones' brow lifted. "I admire your resolve, General, but we still haven't told you the actual mission."

Wentz stalled. "I assumed that the mission is, well, to test fly the OEV."

"Not exactly," Ashton admitted. "There's something else you need to know, sir. It's much more important than you, me, the OEV—it's more important than anything."

"That's why we need you," Jones added, "and that's why we need you now."

A long silence hung over the office. Wentz sat there, waiting.

"Are you gonna tell me or do I have to guess?"

It was the sudden solemnness of Jones and Ashton that most bothered Wentz. He didn't like the feeling at all.

"Follow me please, General."

Wentz followed Jones out while Ashton paused for the slightest moment, then likewise left the in-briefing room.

Wentz didn't see her pop the tiny pill in her mouth.

———————

Jones led them down another antiseptically white corridor lined with white key-padded doors. A maintenance tech at one of the doors began to snap to attention but Jones sluffed, "As you were, as you were, Sergeant."

The tech was about to paint something on the door, and Wentz couldn't help but notice. Shiny black letters on the door read: BRIGADIER GENERAL W. FARRINGTON, but then the tech painted over the W. FARRINGTON and raised a stencil that read J. WENTZ.

"You guys are a scream," Wentz said, chuckling. "But I'm telling you, you can hard-sell me all day long but I'm still retiring tomorrow."

Ashton and Jones said nothing.

Jones unlocked another door, marked simply CONFERENCE. Inside, Wentz noticed several chart graphs and murals, as if for a presentation. One mural seemed to be an artist's depiction of some sort of space-flight mission. A bulletin board read:

-QSR4 JOINT JAPAN/RUSSIAN
    SAMPLE-RETURN MISSION
-SCHEDULE COURSE AND
    PERIHELIC TRAJECTORY
    (EST. 62,700,000 MILES).
-PROJECTED COST (US EQ.)
    $34 BILLION
-PROJECTED TIME
    EXPENDITURE (IN FLIGHT):
    19 MONTHS.

Wentz sat down, ready to listen.

Jones began, "When the so-called Mars Meteor, designate ALH-84001, was found in August, 1996, and…well, you remember the news."

"Sure," Wentz recalled. "Fossilized microbacteria, fairly solid proof that there was rudimentary, one-celled life on Mars, something like 3.5 billion years ago."

"Yes. After which every country in the world with space flight capability began to draw up plans for further investigations of the Martian surface. The ultimate end, of course, is a sample/return mission—quite sophisticated and very expensive, but this would enable a robotic surface device to collect soil samples, which would later be returned to Earth by way of a staged orbiter rocket sent afterwards…"

"QSR4 is the codename for one such plan," Ashton augmented, "and it's already in service—"

Wentz pinched his chin. "I haven't heard about any—"

"No, you haven't, General, and neither has the rest of the world. The Japanese agreed to finance the Russian Space Administration on the mission you see outlined on the mural."

81

"Why would the Japanese bankroll the Russians? Our aerospace technology is better than theirs."

"Not so much as you think," Jones said, "and, additionally, no other space administration in the world trusts us. They all think we've got field operatives planting discreet probe-implants and sensors on all their space hardware."

Wentz looked duped. "Why would they think that?"

"Well...because it's true. We've been doing it for decades — saves us lots of money. Why send up our own missions when we can tap and analyze *their* findings?"

"Cloak and Dagger is alive and well," Wentz supposed. "The United States — the world's best friend."

Ashton ignored the sarcasm. "General, a year ago, the joint Japanese/Russian mission was initiated. A collection probe — QSR4 — landed in the Tharsus Bulge on Mars and immediately began to relay findings back to Earth—"

"And to *us*," Wentz finished, "from the taps we secretly planted in their probe."

"Yes. And what the collector discovered was more than bacterial fiber fossils but...*live* bacteria."

"You're not joking, are you?" Wentz asked.

"No, General, we're not," Jones said. "The mission's analysis sensors positively identified the organisms as *live*. Our own analysis of the data, however, unbeknownst to the Japanese and the Russians, indicates quite a bit more. Our own spectrographic survey of the probe's findings was processed through CDC and Langley, and the bacteria reveals characteristics consistent with a cytomegalic mutation."

Wentz frowned. "Do I look like a microbiologist?"

Ashton crossed her legs in the chair. "What he means, sir, is that the CDC analysis of the molecular specs strongly suggests that the Tharsus bacteria is host to a virus more hazardous than anything ever found on Earth."

Wentz stared at them through a dark interlude.

"In about six months," Jones went on, "the return stage of the QSR4 mission is going to pick up that collector and bring it back to Earth."

"So tell them to scrub the pickup," Wentz made the most obvious suggestion. "I think if you told them they were bringing a deadly virus back to Earth, they wouldn't have to think long before they aborted the entire mission."

"We can't do that, General. That would acknowledge what they've suspected all along—that our own agents have been planting tap-sensors in their probes. It would ruin foreign relations."

Wentz almost laughed. "Well then *fuck* foreign relations. This is a bit more important, isn't it?"

"It's not that simple, sir," Ashton said.

Wentz considered this. "Fine, then do what you Big Brother guys do best. Destroy the return stage before it gets back—"

"That's even less serviceable," Jones countered. "It would be plainly detectable as a hostile attack on the geostatic DPS net. They'd never believe it was an accident, and since the U.S. is the only country in the world with the sufficient anti-satellite technology to pull something like that off—"

"They'd know it was us," Wentz agreed.

"And considering the upcoming trade agreements pending in Congress," Ashton reminded, "we'd lose all economic ties with the Japanese forever, and the Russians would more than likely freeze all U.S. investment assets currently in place."

"So you see our dilemma," Jones said. "If we sabotage their return mission on its way back, we risk an economic war that could put us in a true depression. And if we tell them of our knowledge of the nature of the bacteria—that we've secretly installed the equivalent of analytical eaves-dropping devices on their space missions, then the news will hit every wire service in the world, and we'll lose every ally we have."

Wentz couldn't believe the nit-picking here. "What are you guys? Republicans? You consider positive U.S. foreign relations more important than preventing a potential plague?"

"It wouldn't be a *potential* plague, sir," Ashton explained. "All the spectrographic and chromatographic analysis of the data we intercepted from the QSR4 sample-collector indicates a viral component with exponential contagion attributes. If that return stage succeeds in bringing the Tharsus bacteria back to Earth—"

Jones' voice grated, "Millions, and potentially *billions*, could die. A virus like that...could wipe out all mammalian life on the planet."

Wentz shook his head in complete outrage. "So like I just told you. To hell with foreign relations and the economy. This is *more important*. Tell them. Admit that we've been slipping taps on their space-flight missions and tell them to abort the damn return stage."

"Again," Jones said, "it's not quite that simple. Don't you read the papers?"

"Hell, no," Wentz said. "They're all biased. I watch Fox News, that's it."

"Well, then, you might be aware that the Russian parliament is squeezing the executive branch to sign a non-aggression pact with Red China."

"Sure, but it'll never happen. Yeltsin would never bend to that. He'd disband the entire parliament first. He'd shut down the government."

"Not if he's dead," Ashton said. "And not if his government is replaced."

Wentz's eyes narrowed. "I guess you people know something I don't."

"Yeltsin's government is on the verge of collapse," Jones said. "The opposition parties have been trying to kill him for two years. That last heart attack? It wasn't natural causes. A radical element of the GRU managed to get some potassium dichlorate in his food. It was a U.S. team of cardiologists from Johns Hopkins that saved his life. The fact of the matter is, Yeltsin won't last till Christmas; his government will topple."

Ashton again: "And whatever party takes over will sign the pact with Red China because it's the easiest way to cut defense funding and pump it into the economy, avoid a revolution. China is still technically our enemy, and if they sign a pact with Russia?"

"Russia becomes a potential enemy again too," Wentz realized. "And the Cold War starts all over again."

Jones stood up, aiming a wooden pointer at the mural depicting the QSR4's return trip to Earth. "Exactly, and if Russia and Red China become allies…what do you think they'll do if they find out that return-stage is bringing back a virus deadlier than anything the planet has ever known?"

Wentz's eyes widened to the size of slot-machine slugs. "They might *not* abort the stage. They might let it return and retrieve it." Wentz's throat went dry. "They might try to contain the virus."

"That's right, General," Ashton said. "They might try to contain it, and preserve it as a weapon."

"A weapon we'd have no defense against," Jones tacked on.

Ashton looked right into Wentz's eyes. "So, General, we're asking you to undertake a mission which would circumvent what is potentially the worst catastrophe in human history, an event that could wipe out the human race…"

CHAPTER 9

"They're always best when you catch them yourself," Pete said, then smacked a claw with the wooden mallet.

"They sure are," Joyce Wentz agreed. The kitchen swam in spicy aromas of Old Bay and vinegar. A quick glance out the window showed the yard darkening, the sun down. It was nearing 9 p.m. "And you did a great job cooking them," she added. "These are the best I've had."

The heap of cooked crabs lay on the newspaper-covered table. They were starting to get cool. Joyce suspected that her son knew full well that she was placating him—anything to avoid the issue. Soon she couldn't think of anything to say as they sat there in silence plucking tender white crabmeat. The hardest part was simply containing her rage.

The son of a bitch should've at least called...

Pete finished his third crab; usually he ate six or eight. Eventually he said, "I guess Dad's not coming back tonight, huh, Mom?"

"Probably not."

"But he did say he's retiring tomorrow, right? He said for us to be there at noon."

"That, right, that's what he said."

"I guess he just had some last-minute things to do at the base, secret papers to sign and all."

"That's probably it, Pete," Joyce said, struggling for all she was worth to hold back the tears of her anger. *That son of a bitch! He's got no right to do this to us!*

Pete stood up, his shirt flecked with specks of red spice. He began to transfer the rest of the crabs to a big platter. "I'll put the rest in the fridge. Dad'll want some tomorrow after his retirement ceremony."

More silence then. Joyce tempered herself, picking up the kitchen. She hoisted the black-enameled crab pot to the sink, prepared to clean it.

"I'll do that, Mom," Pete said after he put the crabs away. "Dad always says, the guy who messes up the kitchen cleans the kitchen."

"No, honey, you go ahead. Your shows are coming on. I'll clean up."

"Thanks, Mom!" Pete turned to head for the TV room but stopped short. "Oh, and I was thinking. I think when I get out of college, I want to join the Air Force. I want to be a pilot like Dad."

Pete trotted from the room. Moments later, the TV could be heard.

Joyce Wentz unconsciously squeezed the Brillo pad so hard it cut her skin. Her tears plipped into the sink, all the while she kept thinking *That son of a bitch, that goddamn son of a bitch!*

Back in the main hangar, Wentz, Ashton, and Jones strolled idly around the OEV. It's temporary paint job was done, the maintenance techs gone.

"It's your duty, General," Jones said. "There's no other choice, and there's no one more qualified."

Wentz stared at the craft. "Jesus… You want me to fly this thing to friggin' *Mars*, and then—

And destroy the QSR4 collector," Ashton explained. "When it stops relaying its navigational signals, the Japanese and the Russians will terminate the return stage. Sixty-five million miles away they can't possibly suspect sabotage on our part. They'll deduce that a tectonic fault or crustic surface quake destroyed the collector. They'll have nothing to bring back and no way to investigate."

But Wentz only partially understood. "Fly to Mars, blow up a probe. But you know something, folks? I don't see any Hellfires or Mavericks on this thing..."

"Externally mounted bombs or missiles aren't possible," Jones specified. "Even if we could find a way to attach some hard-points to the exterior hull, any ordnance would break apart or even detonate once the OEV accelerated past light speed."

Wentz hadn't considered that. "Which means—"

"Which means you'll have to touch down and debark on foot."

"The alien air-lock works perfectly, sir," Ashton assured him. "We've even posted directions. You close the bottom port, you hit a press-panel and wait thirty seconds, then open the hatch and climb out."

Wentz felt a few shimmies in his gut. "You want me to EVA on *Mars*?"

"Why not?" Jones passed it off as if discussing a stroll to the supermarket. "You'll be wearing NASA's top-of-the line gear. And you'll have plenty of time to set the charge before the surface temperature compromises the suit's life support systems."

"What's the temperature?" Wentz dared ask.

"This time of year? About 190 below zero," Ashton informed him.

Wentz glared at her. "And I thought Syracuse was bad."

Now the silence in the hangar felt like pressure. Wentz looked dolefully at the strange, heel-shaped vehicle.

"I don't have to ask any more, do I, General Wentz?" Jones inquired.

"Of course not. A virus that could kill everyone on the planet? What choice do I have?"

"We're glad you realize the severity of the circumstances."

"But hear this, major. I pull *this job* and that's it. After I come back, I'm out. I retire. Hell, my ex-wife's given me three breaks—maybe she'll give me a fourth."

Ashton leaned against the OEV's hull, her head bowed down. Jones rubbed his temples as if groping for an excuse not to meet Wentz's gaze.

"What the fuck is *this* now?" Wentz asked.

"It's...far more complicated than that," Jones made the arcane statement. "You see, sir..."

"What?"

"It's not as simple as completing the mission and out-processing."

"Why? You want me for the gig, I said I'd do it."

"There are...exigencies, sir, and—"

Wentz felt his temper flaring again. "I don't even know what the fuck that means. Quit babbling and give me the scoop."

"Once you complete the mission, there's no returning to civilian life...no returning to your family. The implications toward national security wouldn't permit that."

Wentz's heart rate doubled at once, and his patience left the hangar. "You little Wally Cleaver-looking motherfucker!" and then Wentz grabbed Jones by his crisp Air Force collar and slammed him against the OEV's hull. "I had a TS/SI clearance when you were still playing with army men. You've got balls implying that I'd ever, EVER, break my secrecy oath, you little piece of—"

"Release the Major!" a voice shouted. In seconds, one of the sentries had rushed forward, and had a service pistol to Wentz's head. "Release the Major now, sir!"

Wentz did no such thing. He tightened his grip on Jones' collar, their faces an inch apart. "I'm sick to death of little Tekna/Byman pissants like you shitting on me. You know how many times I've been polygraphed and narco-analyzed, you asshole? I've *never* divulged restricted information, to *anyone*—"

The sentry shouted, "Release the Major right now, or I'll have to kill you, sir!" The sentry cocked his pistol.

Then, propped up against a UFO with Wentz's hands around his neck, Jones shouted back the strangest thing. "Stand down!" he yelled at the sentry. "Holster your pistol and return to your post! That's an order!"

The sentry, flabbergasted, lowered his weapon and backed off.

But Wentz didn't budge. "You think I'm gonna fly to *Mars* and then go home and tell my wife about it? What the fuck is wrong with you? No one's got the right to question my loyalty to my country—"

"No one's questioning your loyalty or service, sir," Ashton said. "No one's implying that you'd breach your secrecy oaths. You're over-reacting. Let him down."

Wentz cooled off one degree, and released Jones.

Winded, pink-faced, collar ripped, Jones did a fairly bad job of regaining his composure. "Jesus, General—"

"Then quit fucking with me," Wentz growled.

Ashton touched Wentz's arm. "Come with me, sir. For the last block of your briefing."

Another blazing white corridor, then another sterile briefing room. Wentz and Ashton sipped coffee under humming fluorescent light. Whatever this was about, Wentz knew it was serious. Minutes ticked by before Ashton finally broke the silence: "As you've probably ascertained, sir, there's one more catch."

"I kind of figured."

"But you do realize the gravity of the situation, don't you?"

"Yes!" he snapped.

Ashton didn't react. "Operator compatibility with the OEV's guidance and navigational systems requires certain...alterations."

Wentz looked up quizzically over his coffee. "What, system alterations?"

"No, sir. I don't mean alterations to the vehicle itself. I mean alterations...to the operator."

Wentz's thoughts froze. *The operator?*

"*Surgical* alterations," Ashton finished.

Morosely, then, she passed Wentz a glossy 8x10 photograph.

Wentz stopped breathing for a moment.

The photo showed two scarred, deformed human hands. Index and pinkie fingers gone, the web of the thumb gone, the middle and ring fingers widely separated.

Human hands with only three fingers each.

"God in heaven," Wentz muttered, his eyes pulled open by shock.

"That is a post-op photograph of General Farrington's hands," Ashton dryly stated. "It was taken three weeks after the required procedure."

"This is crazy," Wentz said just as dryly.

"The operator detents—the handprints—will not function unless the pilot's hands are an *exact, morphological fit*."

Next she showed him another photo: Farrington's three-fingered hands pressed into the detent outlines in the OEV's control panel.

"It's absolutely essential," Ashton went on. "There's no other possible way to operate the OEV without first undergoing the procedure. We've tried every conceivable alternative. None of them worked."

"What alternatives?" Wentz mouthed, still looking wide-eyed at the pictures.

"A number of Army and Navy demolition men who'd lost two fingers on each hand in training accidents. Then there was a flight technician from McCord who'd lost two fingers while working on the flap-servos of a C-141. He volunteered to have his good hand altered too but, again, it didn't work. We've even brought down some civilians with tridactylism, a rare genetic defect in which the afflicted are born with only three fingers on each hand. None of it worked."

Wentz got up, stormed around the room. "I can't go back to my wife and kid with hands like that!"

"No, General, you can't. And due to the aggressiveness of the procedure, there's no way to effect a cosmetic reversal. The surgery requires a complete removal of the index and pinkie fingers along with their adjoining metacarpals, removal of the web of flesh between the index finger and thumb, and a 21-degree widening of the phalange-margin between the middle and ring fingers."

Wentz's anger impacting with his incomprehension felt like someone hitting him in the head with a hammer.

"There's *no other way*, sir. Without the surgical modifications, the necessary conduction of the pilot's brain waves cannot be synaptically transferred to the OEV's systems..."

"Well what about those other guys?" Wentz rebelled. "What happened with them?"

"Absolutely nothing. The palmar alignments weren't concise enough to achieve a positive connection with the detents."

I'm not gonna do this, he thought. *I've got a wife and kid.* But then the rest of the consideration took root. *If that sample-collector comes back to Earth…they'd die, I'd die, maybe everyone would die.*

"There is no other recourse, sir," Ashton said.

"I know."

"So you're going to do it, right?"

Wentz nodded. "Yes."

"Your wife and your son will be personally notified—"

"Some cover story, I suppose. The old empty casket."

"Yes. They'll be told that you were killed in a test crash."

It was only darkness now that filled his mind, and blazing regrets. "Joyce and I are still technically divorced. I need to make sure she gets everything, and all of my SOM pay."

"JAG will take care of all that, sir."

Wentz lowered his face into his hands, tears suddenly slipping from his eyes.

"I'll be back later to show you to your quarters, General," Ashton said. Then she quietly left the room.

The next day, the banquet room of the Thornsen Center stood crowded with Air Force personnel in their Class-A's, their wives, their children. The base commander and several other generals milled about impatiently. The entire auditorium seemed like a congregation with no purpose. Something stiff and uncomfortable throbbed through the air.

Civilian caterers in white hats traded pinched looks behind tables stacked with refreshments and steam tables.

Above the stage, where the retirement presentation was to be held, hung a long sign which read CONGRATULATIONS, JACK WENTZ!

"This is so fucked up I can't believe it," 1st Sergeant Caudill muttered.

"I hear ya, Top," Sergeant Cole agreed. He glanced at his watch. "He's more than an hour late for his own retirement. I don't get it."

"Neither do I—shit, there's his wife." Top, with considerable reluctance, approached Mrs. Joyce Wentz and her son, who seemed to be wending their way toward the exit door.

"I don't know what to tell you, Mrs. Wentz," Top offered. "Maybe he got the day wrong or something. I can't believe he'd miss this."

"I can. We're leaving now, Sergeant."

"Well, wait, ma'am. Maybe he just got tied up, maybe he just—"

"Goodbye, Sergeant."

Mrs. Wentz turned, holding her son's hand.

"He's not coming, is he, Mom?"

"No, Pete. I'm sorry. Let's go home now."

Top watched them both leave the auditorium. He glanced at his watch again and grimaced, edging back to where Cole stood.

"All this time I thought he was a great guy," Top remarked.

"Some great guy. Looks like he dumped his own retirement party and skated on his wife and kid."

"How do you like that?" Caudill said. "Wentz turned out to be an A-one prick."

"I'm a freak now," the words grated a day later.

It was Wentz who'd uttered them, propped up in the hospital bed of Area S-4's medical unit. The surgery had taken almost ten hours, and now he lay in a pain-killer fog.

He held up his two braced and bandaged hands—hands with only three fingers each.

"I'm a monster…"

When the door clicked open and Ashton entered, Wentz quickly slipped his hands beneath the bed sheets.

"There's nothing to be ashamed about, sir. What you've done is heroic."

Wentz glanced away. "Leave me alone, will you?"

"The healing and recovery process will only take a few weeks. After that a week of physical therapy. Then, when you're…comfortable with, uh—"

"With my new hands? My ruined, scarred, hideous hands?"

"—you'll alternately train on the OEV and participate in some EVA simulations, some simple training blocks on field demolitions. etc. Believe it or not, General, the worst part is over."

Wentz boomed, "Yeah? Tell that to my wife and kid! I'll never see them again! My wife'll hate me! My kid'll grow up thinking I'm a lying piece of garbage who didn't love him! Now get out!"

Ashton sullenly left the room.

CHAPTER 18

For the next month, about the only sound Wentz remained cognizant of was the tick of the clock. Time.

Time was life.

His quarters, his office, every briefing room and every training cove—there was a general issue Air Force clock on the wall, ticking.

The tick of the clock sounded like dripping blood.

Every night when he slept, the commitment he'd made dug his heart out. He knew he was doing the only thing he *could* do, but there was no solace in that, not at night when he was alone. He dreamed of teaching Pete how to drive the new dirt bike, he dreamed of Pete's high school graduation, sending him off to the prom, sending him off to college, and all of the other things he, Wentz, would never really see.

He dreamed of making love to Joyce...

All lost, all ashes.

And then he'd waken, in darkness. He'd bring his hands to his clenched face, but the hands only had three fingers on each. And then he'd hear it.

He'd hear the only thing in the world that never changed: the tick of the clock.

tick tick tick

drip drip drip

S-4 had a psychiatrist and occupational therapist. Both Ashton and "Jones" urged him to see them—"to adjust to the necessary period of mental and physical refraction," Jones had said—but Wentz said "Fuck that shit. I don't need any damn shrinks. I'm a U.S. Air Force Senior Test, I'm not a nut."

He knew what he'd done, he knew what level his duty had taken him to (and he knew why). So Wentz did what he always had.

He did his job.

He spent a week on Unisys flight simulators, programmed for the OEV. It was cake. Two more days training with demolition-block material, fuses, detcord, blasting caps and primers. Eight hours a day for a week bobbing in a cylindrical water tank for zero-gravity familiarization, then several sessions in the cargo hold of a C-131 nose-diving from 40,000 feet to 5,000 feet (the latter was fun, the former...not so fun). Another cake-walk was the MMU training. An MMU (for Manned Mobility Unit) was NASA's latest, state-of-the-art "space suit"—over $10,000,000 per suit.

Wentz dug it.

Days lapsed as they always had in the past, a new joyride, a new thrill. Duty, yes, but the adrenalin always made it better. At forty-five years old, Wentz scored higher on the spirometer, the MMPA, the MMU field test, and the technical diagnostic batteries than most of the country's active astronauts.

"Looks like you're ready, General," one of the training tests told him.

"You think?" Wentz had answered. "It might look like it, but this ain't a lug-wrench in my pants, son."

No, even a day after the surgery, Wentz never doubted himself. He was going to this job like he'd done every job in his career.

The *best* job.

His "shit" was "square."

And on the day before his first live test flight of the OEV, unfazed by the deformity of his hands, General Jack Wentz looked straight in the mirror with a leveled eye and said: "Hardcore. I'm fuckin' there."

Yes, that was how the days went. He was the best pilot in the world, and they were great days.

The only thing that bothered him were the nights. When he'd dream and later wake up to the sound of dripping blood...

Wentz sat strapped into the operator's seat, a modified job by Hughes Aircraft. He wore a visorless helmet and standard Air Force jumpsuit. Ashton wore the same, sitting beside him.

They felt the modest vibration as the platform elevator lifted them up thirteen nuke-proof levels through this underground complex.

When Ashton glanced at his bare, three-fingered hands, he moved them away.

"Don't be self-conscious, sir. It could debilitate you, it could degrade your performance."

"I'm not gonna fuck up your goddamn UFO," he snapped back. He looked at her with a sly grin. "I'm gonna fly this thing better than Farrington ever dreamed."

"Fine. Don't talk about it. Do it."

Bitch, he thought. *I'll show her ass.*

The elevator droned upward, then shuddered to a stop.

"This is a daylight test flight," she reminded. "This is strictly familiarization. Fly slow, fly stable. This first run is just for you to get the feel of the OEV. If you fly too fast in daylight, you'll burn the camouflage paint off the hull, then we could be spotted by the KH-12 and Russian surveillance satellites."

"Yeah," he said. "I hear ya."

The elevator had lifted them up into a hangar-shaped structure, covered with sand. Just another dune.

Then the dune began to open.

Wentz glimpsed the beautiful desert beyond. The hangar door held open like a stretched jaw.

"Go for it, General. Place your hands into the detents...and fly."

Even after all of the simulations, Wentz froze for a moment. All of his instincts were different now—

"Raise the craft and move forward out of the hangar," Ashton said.

"I know!"

No stick, no throttle.

"Give me a sec," he said.

"Let your mind do the work, sir. We can go back down if you're apprehensive, give it another shot tomorrow."

Bitch, he thought again.

And then he let his mind do the work.

Wentz lightened the pressure of his hands into the detents. He *thought*.

Immediately a dark garnet-tinged light filled the interior, behind a very low sub-octave *thrumming* sound. Then the craft raised a foot off the elevator platform and began to move forward out of the hangar.

"Good. You're doing it."

"Charlie-Oscar, this is Jonah One," Ashton transmitted from her CVC mike. "Request permission for take-off."

"Roger, Jonah One. Permission granted."

Wentz eased the OEV fully out of the hangar. *It's working,* he thought, dumbfounded. *I don't believe it...* He moved the entire craft out into the high, sweltering sun. Beyond the OEV's strange windows, the desert shimmered. Wentz remained in partial stasis as the craft just sat there and hovered.

Behind them, the opening to the phony sand dune drew closed.

Wentz gazed at the desert.

"General, we can sit here all day if you like," Ashton said. "You're the boss, you know? But I kind of thought that you might want to do something other than hover."

"Oh. Yeah," Wentz replied.

Then the OEV essentially disappeared from its former stance. There was no roar of an engine being throttled to the max. There was no inertia crushing them back into their seats. There was only sky which, within minutes, faded away as Wentz took the OEV out of Earth's proper atmosphere.

Within minutes, they were in space.

Wentz could feel his mind become *part* of the vehicle, like a jump board, like a guidance microprocessor. The processor was Wentz's *brain*, and his brain's connectivity to the rest of the ship were his hands pressed into the detents.

"Damn it, General!" Ashton snipped.

"What? You told me to get moving, so...I got moving."

"I expected a little discipline. This is a first test run. It's a familiarization sortie, for you to get the hang of the OEV's basic navigational possibilities. I told you not to accelerate too drastically, so not to burn the paint off the hull. You've just shot us out of orbit!"

"Hey, paint's cheap," Wentz said.

"Maybe, sir, but since you've burned it all off in a hyper-velotic cruise, that means we can't return to the atmosphere until after sundown—six hours. Otherwise the satellites might see us."

Wentz chuckled. "Six hours? In *this* rig? I could do sixty before I started to get tired. We're *cruisin'*, Colonel. And I'm the driver. So just sit back and enjoy it."

An endless scape of stars stretched before them.

You gotta be shitting me, Wentz thought, staring outward.

For the last twenty-five years, he was limited to the sky. Now he had the entire universe.

In only a week, Wentz learned to operate the OEV to a degree that he thought there was nothing he—or it—could not do. It was all a mind-set, not that different from a high-tech fighter, the only difference being that the detents reduced reaction time to zero. His brain no longer needed to command his hands on the controls.

Instead—now—his brain was plugged into the aircraft.

Not only could Wentz command the OEV with his mind, he could *tease* it, *jink* it, execute maneuvers that would not have been possible by stick-control or fly-by-wire. The physical human body was simply not capable...but with Wentz's *mind* functioning as an integral component of the OEV's flight systems—

Wentz couldn't imagine the full-scale possibilities.

Barrel-rolls in space, true-toe vertical thrusts, FLOTs and FEBAs and flat-spins and "skidder-turns." Wentz performed aerial moves, within the atmosphere and without, that were unprecedented.

At least by a human.

He wondered how he'd fare compared to the *true* pilots of this vehicle.

"What were they like?" he asked on his seventh test flight. He was encircling the Earth at a 23,000-mile geostatic orbit-track. He wasn't sure—because the OEV had no true-speed indicators, altimeters, or azimuth gauges—but it seemed that each revolution took but seconds. The harder he thought, the faster he went.

"The native operators?" Ashton asked.

"Yeah. Little green men? Silver skin? Big black almond-shaped eyes?"

"I don't know," Ashton confessed, "because I never had a need to. I only know they were air-breathers, bipedal, and warm-blooded. One of the bodies was cryolized, and the other was autopsied, at Wright-Patterson."

"Why do you think they came to Earth?"

"Who knows? A field survey, probably. Probably monitoring our technological progress with regards to weapons of mass destruction. The Edgewood Arsenal? You don't *even* want to know what kind of stuff we've got stored there."

"You're right," Wentz said. "I don't want to know." Wentz took his three-fingered hands out of the detents, leaving his last guidance thoughts in the system: continue following the orbit-line. "How far advanced do you think they are?"

"Probably a thousand years, something like that."

Christ…

"The seal of the egression hatch is so minute, we couldn't even get molecular wire to run a patch to the outer-hull," Ashton remarked. "And even if we could, the hull is impenetrable, no way to mount anything on it." She pointed to the meager bank of readout gauges and VDU's above the detent panel. "A brace-frame holds that stuff in place, same for the storage racks and lockers in back."

"If the hull's impenetrable…how do we have radio contact with S-4?" Wentz asked.

"Luck. Radio waves pass through without any detectable distortion. It's just a standard SINGARS radio we've got installed… You hungry?"

"Sure."

Ashton unhooked her safety belt, walking normally to the rear of the craft, in spite of its tremendous speed and gyrations.

When Wentz wasn't looking, she popped a small pill into her mouth.

Moments later, she returned to her seat, bearing two packs of MRE's.

"Ah, Meals, Ready to Eat," Wentz recognized the o.d.-green wrappers. "You got a hot dogs and beans there?"

"Live it up, sir," she said, and passed him the pack. "And you can have my chocolate disk—"

"The hockey puck?" Wentz exclaimed. "Shit, in the field, guys would sell those things for fifty bucks! You don't want yours?"

Ashton passed him the green cellophane packet, which read CHOCOLATE, ONE (1) DISK, 104 GRAMS. "I don't eat chocolate," Ashton said in a vehicle that was probably surpassing 250,000 miles per hour. "It makes my face break out."

Later test flights would prove equally flawless. Wentz flew to the moon, the Alpha- Centauri double-star system, to Venus.

On the moon, he EVA'd, performing several familiarization sessions in the most technologically advanced "space suit" known to man.

This is a trip, he thought, skipping through dust and an age-old volcanic ejecta in the Aristarchus plains. He picked up an oblong rock close to the shape of a football; he threw it and watched it disappear.

Eat my shorts, John Elway, he thought. *You ain't shit.*

The next day, Wentz was cleared for the mission.

CHAPTER 11

"I love you," Wentz whispered.

"I love you too," Joyce whispered back. Hotly.

His hands molded against her soft flesh; her perfect breasts swayed above his face. Her beautiful dark visage lowered, to kiss him, and Wentz was swept away. His life, for the first time, was perfect.

As he penetrated her, moving with her pleasure, he raised his hands to caress her face—

And when she saw them—his hands, his mutilated, three-fingered hands shiny with scar tissue—

She screamed.

She screamed and pulled away, crawling backward. She began to vomit as she fell off the bed. Wentz lurched up, crawling toward her, and at that same moment, the bedroom door clicked open, and Pete peered in.

"Dad, what—"

"Close the door!" Wentz shouted, pointing at his son.

Pete screamed when he glimpsed his father's hands.

The door slammed shut.

When Wentz looked over the edge of the bed, he saw that his wife had turned into a swollen, vermiculated corpse. Eyes popped and running with fluid. Her skin blue-green. Lumpen bile slipping from her once-pert, now-rotten lips.

"I hate you," the corpse gargled. "I hate you, and so does your son…"

When Wentz came awake, he was gagging at the remnant dream-stench of death.

Fuck, he thought. *This ain't making it…*

The wall clock ticked. Just past 4 a.m.

Four hours, he thought.

He showered, shaved, donned his service whites. He zipped up his leather mitts. When he left his quarters, silence seemed to stalk his footfalls. Level Thirteen was a white labyrinth with no vanishing point. Eventually, he found himself in the OEV vault. The sentries in the shadows didn't move; Wentz felt alone, which was what he wanted. He paced around the OEV, not looking at it as much as looking at his life. He thought about Joyce, he thought about Pete, he thought about all the things he would miss now, but then remembered there was no alternative. There never had been.

The training blocks and the test blocks all seemed unreal now. They were distant dreams; they were like stories someone had told him. When he tried to see the six weeks in his mind…it wasn't him in the operator's seat of the OEV. It was someone else. A dream man.

But today was no dream. His hands had three fingers each. That was real. And in a few hours he would be using those hands—and the instincts they were connected to—to pilot an extraterrestrial vehicle to Mars.

This was real.

Wentz stared at the OEV. They'd had to repaint it each and every time he'd taken it out.

It looked surreal with its desert-sand paint on the top, and the heather-blue on the bottom.

All at once, Wentz couldn't believe what he was looking at, nor what he was about to do in just a few hours.

105

He looked at his watch...

Oh, man...

What felt like twenty minutes had stretched to four hours. It was 0758.

The vault door clanked, then began to rise. Bright white light spilled into the hangar and a figure stood in stark-black silhouette.

Major "Jones" stepped out of the light.

"General, it's time for you to get to the ready room. Time to suit up."

Wentz could hear his watch ticking. "Yeah. I guess it is."

A pressure-suit wasn't necessary; the OEV maintained flawless cabin pressure of 14.7 psi or exactly 100 kilopascals, close to identical to Earth conditions at sea level. In the past, Wentz had worn a simple simulator helmet, since Ashton had monitored the SINGARS radio channels.

"I need a CVC helmet," Wentz informed Jones, "for commo."

"No, you don't, sir," Jones replied.

Another silhouette emerged from the bulkhead light. It was Ashton, dressed in the same flight suit series as Wentz.

"You're coming?" Wentz asked.

"No offense, sir," she said. "You may be the best pilot in the world, but considering you've got a sixty-five-million-mile trip ahead of you, you might need a communications officer."

"Cool with me." Wentz extended his mittened hand toward the OEV. "Hop in."

Wentz climbed up the trolley ladder. He slapped the exterior press-panel.

The top hatch hissed open.

"Let's get this spam can rolling," Wentz said.

106

"Charlie-Oscar, this is Jonah One. Request permission to take off."

The topside door stood yawning open. Bright sky glared beyond.

"Roger, Jonah One. You are cleared."

Fuck this fucking around, Wentz thought. Hands to detents, he jerked the OEV from the hangar entrance...and disappeared.

"Time to cook," he said.

Clouds sailed by, then so did the rest of the atmosphere. Moments later, they were plunged into star-flecked space.

"Is it me, or does this thing fly faster each time we go out?"

"Yes, sir," Ashton responded, "though we haven't come up with a technically sound hypothesis as to why."

"The first time I went up, it seemed to take a lot longer to get out of the atmosphere," Wentz observed.

"And maybe you weren't paying attention, but your second trip to the moon took half as long as your first."

"I can't figure it. There's no throttle, no fuel-flow, no type of velocity controls—"

"It's all in your mind," Ashton asserted. "That's our guess, sir. General Farrington experienced the same thing. Each excursion to the Alpha Cent cluster consumed fewer flying hours. Increased confidence of the operator probably has something to do with it, and familiarization, too. The more flight-hours racked up on the OEV, the greater the feel you have with its total function. The more you get to know it, the faster it flies."

Wentz's brow furrowed. "It sounds like you're telling me I'm having a relationship with a spaceship."

"In a sense, sir, you are. When you put your hands into the detents, you become connected to the vehicle, you become *part*

107

of it. Given the sophistication of technology involved, it's not inaccurate to say that you're bonding with some systemological aspect of the craft."

"Bonding, huh? Guess it's only a matter of time before I start buying it roses."

Ashton remained serious. "Think about it, sir. It only makes sense. A guidance and propulsion system that *connects* to the operator's thought processes? When you become part of the vehicle, it only stands to reason that the vehicle becomes part of you."

Wentz didn't know if he was buying that one, and he preferred not to consider it. The mere fact that he was piloting a craft made by an alien race was hard enough to reckon.

By now, he had learned that a cleanly focused thought was enough to keep the OEV headed on a base trajectory. He needn't keep his hands in the detents at all times.

Wentz removed his hands from the panel, and reached for his gloves.

"You don't need to do that, sir," Ashton said. "Not on my account."

"Yeah? What about *my* account?" he sniped back and slipped on his mitts. "You ever think of that?"

"General, if you're uncomfortable about your hands—"

"Oh, yeah, there's the right word. Uncomfortable. Try appalled. Try disgusted. I'm a freak, Colonel Ashton."

"No, you're not." Ashton's voice was cool, stony. "You're an Air Force restricted test pilot. Your job is to discharge your duty for your country. You knew the score the first time you re-upped. You've made sacrifices in the past, and you've made a sacrifice now. I've made sacrifices too—to be in this position, we all have. So stop whining about your hands."

Wentz yanked his stare around. "Whining?" He couldn't believe it. "That's easy for you to say. You've got ten fingers, I've only got six!"

"You're whining, sir—"

"I can see our trip to Mars is starting out great."

"—and you're jeopardizing the integrity of the mission."

"How's that...*toots*?"

The same cool voice answered, "By allowing yourself to be inhibited about your hands, you're potentially tainting your mental state. Your mental state *runs* the OEV. If you're inhibited, self-conscious, or depressed, those negative emotions can spill over into the vehicle's efficiency and function."

Wentz was about to rail at her...but then he caught himself, thought about what she'd said.

A few moments ticked by.

"And you might want to know, sir," Ashton topped it off. "General Farrington was disciplined enough to *not* be self-conscious about his hands."

Wentz didn't like that, but he also knew what she was doing. *Bitch psychology.* She was leveling Farrington's performance against his.

He unzipped the leather mitts, flung them off. "Who needs gloves anyway?" Then he half-smiled at her. "It's too bad I can't give you the finger..."

———————

"So what's your story?" Wentz asked later, when their tempers had cooled. "Got a husband, kids?"

"No, sir."

"Let me guess. Air Force boyfriend, then, right?"

"No boyfriend," she replied. "That whole scene...it's not for me. Not enough time for a relationship *and* the service. Besides, it's not my style."

"Big bad Air Force girl with super-secret clearance—*that's* your style?"

"Guess so, sir."

Wentz didn't push it. In the window, space streamed by. He realized the impossibility of attaching a true-speed gauge; nevertheless, he was dying to know their approximate velocity. Perhaps telemetry and even the detailed nature of each mission profile regulated when and for how long the OEV would exceed light speed. And perhaps Ashton was correct: maximum performance depended on the psychological attitude of the operator.

"Tell me about Will Farrington," Wentz requested.

"A great man...and an unhappy one," she said. "It all seemed to pile up on him one day. All the things serious pilots leave behind. Wife, children, PTA meetings, the white picket fence."

The words nudged Wentz in the head, like someone palm-heeling him. "So Farrington had a family?"

"Yes, and he didn't think twice about abandoning them. He knew he had to, in order to become Operator 'A.' He deemed it as his duty—just as you have. He did what he had to do because there was no other way. When you consider the utilities of the OEV, its potential for national defense...I'm sure you agree."

Did he? Wentz still wasn't certain. "Are you sure it was *duty* and not just fighter-jock envy? To be honest, I'm still not sure if the reason I took the mission wasn't more for my own ego. Jealousy. Maybe the real reason I'm sitting here with three-fingers on each hand is because I subconsciously couldn't stand the thought of someone else filling this seat. Some Tom-Cruise-looking Navy hammerhead. Some hot shot who's not as good as me."

"I don't think that's the case, sir. And it wasn't the case with General Farrington. In between test runs, he lived at a compound near Andrews. Heavily guarded, mind you. We knew Farrington was becoming depressed because of his TATs, MMPIs, and his digital polygraphs. He actually tried to escape the compound several times. Eventually, we couldn't trust him; we had to put cameras in his suite and a HIR direction-finder on his ankle. And you know what? He *still* escaped."

Escaped? Wentz wondered. *The job must've turned him into a prisoner.* "Why, though? Why did he escape?"

"To see his daughter. She'd been adopted after his wife killed herself. A TACLET squad caught him and brought him back."

Yes, Wentz thought. *A prisoner. Now I'm the prisoner.* Did the same await Wentz once this mission was over? To be locked up in some luxury *suite,* surrounded by guards, beckoned by suicide?

Wentz didn't want to think about it. He didn't want to think about what might happen to his mind five or ten years from now.

"Tell me this, and be honest," he asked, unable to resist. "Was Farrington... Was he better than me?" Wentz looked at her. "Be honest."

"That's really not the point, sir—"

"Tell me!" he barked at her. "That's an order! Was Farrington a better pilot than me?"

Ashton smirked, sighing. "Yes, sir, in my opinion, he was."

Well, I asked for it, and I got it. But why should such insecurities arise now? Wentz knew that Farrington was better, better than anyone in the world. "I guess I should stop acting like a kid and just be happy that I'm second best."

"Be real, sir. You're the second-best pilot in the *world.* That's pretty good."

Wentz nodded. *She's right. I don't see any Navy punks from Miramar flying this thing. I see ME.*

The OEV cruised on, the strange hum in the cabin somehow comforting. Ashton unstrapped and got out of her seat. "I'll be right back. I need to check the APU's and the range-reply readouts."

Wentz shrugged from the pilot's seat. "Why? My brain tells the guidance system where we're going."

"Not if you daydream. Not if you happened to be thinking about Miss July when you were adjusting your trim."

"Aw, Miss July was a dog—"

"Our double-R computer is the only way we can know for sure that we're on course."

Ashton stooped to the rear of the craft where brace-frames mounted the only hardware aboard that was manufactured by human beings. *Here we go again,* Wentz thought. He could see her in the wind-screen's reflection. She knew they were on the proper trajectory; she didn't even look at the range-reply coordinates.

Instead, she reached into a pocket, withdrew a pill, and popped it into her mouth. Over the past month, Wentz had seen her do this several times.

She returned to her commo seat. "I apologize, General. It's clear you weren't thinking about Miss July. Your mental integrity is straight-on."

Wentz wondered what he should do, then he just said it. "Look, Colonel, just because I'm a knucklehead plane driver doesn't mean I'm not observant. What's with the pills you've been popping behind my back?"

Ashton had just strapped back in. Then she looked crestfallen. "Fuck," she whispered.

"Remember what I told you about profanity? Doesn't mix right with all your spit and polish. And what are the pills? Don't tell me Dexatrim 'cos I won't buy it."

"Low-dose Duramorph and MS-Contin," she uttered. "I hate sympathy—I didn't want to tell you."

"Tell me what?"

"I've got bone cancer. Metastatic and inoperable..."

Wentz glanced at her with a trapped expression. "I—Jesus. I'm sorry..."

"Don't be. I just said, I hate sympathy, sir."

Shit, she's so young... "Right, I gotcha. Damn. And quit with the 'sir' and 'general' bit, huh? My name's Jack. You gotta first name besides Colonel?"

"Jill," she said.

Wentz laughed. "No kidding? I love it! Jack and Jill went up the hill...to fly to *fuckin'* Mars!"

Ashton spared a smile herself. "And speaking of Mars, sir—er Jack... There it is."

Wentz's eyes glued to the port-side window. The red sphere grew exponentially, from pea-size in space until it took up Wentz's entire scope of vision.

He pressed his hands back into the detents, then the OEV automatically began to maneuver into a perihelion-descent orbit.

Mars was only red in a telescope, due to refractive occultation from the small planet's diminutive atmosphere and wind systems blowing dust and sublimated vapors of frozen carbon dioxide. This close, the surface of the slightly lopsided planet appeared more like the hue of dull brass. Like streaks of fat through steak, ribbons of more frozen carbon dioxide looked like canals filled with water. Wentz had his hands back in the detents as he cruised the OEV smoothly over peaks, ridges, and crater edges. Wentz rode the planet's jagged surface like a surfer over waves.

It was a good time.

The OEV's system responses amazed him. He could do anything. He could alter trim by two degrees or one hundred and eighty just by a thought. He could turn to fly between crater peaks simply by looking out the window. And it happened.

Fuck, he thought. *I could've ended the Gulf War in one day with this thing.*

From the Air Force gear behind them, something began to beep. "Slow to a crawl," Ashton instructed. "It's our SHF interception of the QSR4's gamma beacon. You know what line-of-sight means. Start looking."

All Wentz saw was the same brass-colored surface. The beeping behind them began to increase.

"Can you imagine if you *hadn't* found out about the virus?" he posed.

"Thank God we did."

"It's incredible that you could identify it all just through intercepted radio waves."

"Not really. It's just digitalized data based on photochemical analysis, spectrography, chromatography."

Wentz figured he should stick with what he knew: flying. "How long till we find this thing and give it the eighty-six?"

"Right about..." Ashton leaned forward in her seat. "This should be it. We're sitting right in the middle of the Tharsus grid-plat."

They both squinted through the prismoid windows.

"There it is!" Ashton exclaimed. "See the tread-marks? Just right of center, one o'clock."

"Uhhhh...yeah! Got it!"

Wentz slowed the OEV, then hovered. Tread-marks in the Martian dust ended at the QRS4 sample-collector. The mechanical probe was about the size of a golf cart on tractor treads. High-gain antennae spired from its top as a small radio dish spun lazily from the front end.

"What's the safe-distance for the RDX charge?" Wentz asked. "A hundred feet?"

"A hundred *meters*. "This is micro-gravity, remember?"

Wentz slowly backed up the OEV while Ashton held a portable rangefinder to her eye, focusing on the probe.

"You're good," she said.

Wentz took his hands out of the detents. He paused a moment, gazing out the window onto this otherworldly landscape.

"No time like the present, right?"

"Go for it," Ashton said.

———————

Fifteen minutes later, Wentz hauled himself out of the OEV's airlock, cumbersome as a tortoise in the bulky white EVA suit. *What a rip-off*, he thought. *I'm the first human being to walk on Mars…and no one will ever know.* He skipped forward away from the craft, each step lifting him inches off the surface. In a gravitational field thirty-eight percent less than Earth, clouds of dust looked like bizarre smoke trailing behind his footfalls. He bounced more than walked toward the tracked probe.

Once he got there, he almost felt disappointed. The probe didn't look like much: a reflective box on treads.

"I'm here," he radioed back to Ashton. "This thing doesn't look like much of a big deal."

"It cost the Russians and Japanese the equivalent of a hundred million dollars, and it cost fourteen *billion* to get it here. They've spent an additional twenty billion to retrieve it."

"Ouch!" Wentz replied. "And now I'm gonna blow it up with a demo charge that probably cost the Army ten bucks. This has to be the most outrageous act of vandalism in the history of humankind."

"That's right," Ashton agreed in his earpiece. "And *you're* the perpetrator!"

"Thanks." Wentz lowered to his knees, fumbling for his carry-satchel. "The ground here is sort of shiny."

"Frozen noble gasses, sublimated argon, probably some good old-fashioned ice," Ashton responded through crackles of mild static.

"Ice, huh? Too bad we didn't bring some Johnny Black and a couple of glasses."

His heavily gloved hands began to remove his demo gear. First came the cone-shaped, olive-drab bomb itself, the size of a coffee thermos. Stenciled letters read: **CHARGE, DEMOLITION, SHAPED (ONE) 2.2 POUNDS, PROPERTY OF U.S. ARMY MUNITIONS COMMAND**. Then he removed a short coil of wire connected to a standard Herco-Tube blasting cap, and a small box- shaped timer with a knob. He placed the charge on the probe, connected the proper wires.

"I think we're ready for the show," he said.

"Set the timer for thirty minutes, then come back."

His bulky hand reached for the broad timer knob but stopped just short of touching it. He was looking up toward the nearest ridge.

Something glinted. "Wait a sec, I see something…near the—"

"It's probably just carbonaceous deposits," Ashton returned. "Forget about it. Come on back."

Wentz squinted through the gold-flaked NASA face-shield. "No, no, it's… I'm gonna check it out."

"Negative, Jack!" Ashton objected. "It could be a plate crack! It could be an ice shelf! You could fall in!"

"I'll take my chances."

116

Ashton's voice shrilled through the static. "Jack—damn it! No! You're violating your orders!"

Fuck orders, Wentz thought.

He bounced away from the probe, moving sluggishly toward the ridge. Once at the edge, he stopped completely, staring down.

"God," he muttered when he realized what he'd seen glinting between the crags.

It was another OEV.

CHAPTER 12

A shton watched Wentz's progress through the range-finder. She clenched a moment, grit her teeth, then shuddered as she reached for another time-released Duramorph. Until recently, she'd been able to control the pain fairly well but now it was just getting worse. Though the doctors recommended higher doses, Ashton wouldn't hear of it. *I'm not going to turn myself into a junkie,* she vowed to herself.

The drug kicked in, lifting her.

By now, Wentz was out of range, and by the time she'd radio composed herself and refocused the range-finder...

"Damn it."

Wentz had already climbed over the edges of the ridge.

Wentz's mind was strangely blank as he climbed onto the second OEV, opened the top- hatch, and lowered himself into the air-lock. The hatch sealed shut above his head and then the chamber decompressed with a familiar swoosh.

Only when he stepped through the egress was he able to think, *Somebody's got some explaining to do...*

He stepped into the cabin, then hit the slidelocks and removed his helmet. The flight seats were empty, but before he could turn around —

"It's...Wentz, isn't it? 41st Test Wing out at Andrews?" a voice queried behind him. "I saw you fly the upgraded 16s at the Paris Air Show in 88—damn good flying."

Stifled, Wentz turned around.

"Welcome to the Tharsus Bulge, Wentz," the voice continued. "My name is—"

Wentz could only stare. He already knew. "You're Willard Farrington, U.S. Marine Corps," he croaked. A pause stretched through the cabin. "Operator 'A.'"

The man looked haggard in his S-4 white jumpsuit as he lay on a fold-down strap bunk. An unkempt beard, trace specks of hair cropping up around the sides of a bald head. Opened packages of MRE's lay like litter about the bunk.

"They told me you were dead," Wentz said flatly. "They told me there was only one of these things."

"They told you a lot of stuff—most of it was a lie." Farrington leaned up in the bunk. He seemed exhausted, or in pain. "What do you expect from the military? You know the game. But—congratulations, Wentz. You earned the ultimate prize, fair and square."

"What do you mean?"

"You truly *are* the best pilot in the world."

"No I'm not, sir. You are."

Farrington chuckled. "The best pilot in the world doesn't *crash* his kite, especially when it's an operational alien spacecraft."

"You crashed? Here?" Wentz was incredulous.

"I sure as shit did," Farrington admitted. "Don't that beat all, with all the nape-of-the-Earth training we get? I came in too low over the first rise, smacked my six right into the ridge and belly-landed here. Still got air and climate-control but—" Farrington pointed toward the detent panels. "No power. All prop systems are deadlined."

119

He wrecked, Wentz realized. "When?"

Farrington shrugged. "About eight weeks ago. That's how long I've been sitting here." Another chuckle. "Can you imagine how pissed off Rainier was when he got the news that I trashed his UFO? Fuck. I feel like the biggest asshole in the history of aviation. I make that meat-head who cracked up his B-2 bomber look like Chuck Yeager."

"You can come back with us," Wentz blurted at the news. "There's enough room."

"You still don't get it, do you? Let me guess. They probably gave you some line about how they identified the virus from intercepted data transmissions or something."

"Yeah... We knew but the Russians and the Japanese didn't because their analysis technology isn't as good as ours."

"Um-hmm. Typical military bullshit. The only thing they knew from the jacked data was that there was live bacteria on the ridge. So they sent me up here to get samples. *I'm* the one who found out it was a virus, and I found out the hard way..."

Farrington pulled up his sleeves: splotches showed on his arms like a glittery, wet rash.

"You're...infected?" Wentz asked.

"That's right. And so are you—the second you debarked. Look at your boots."

Wentz looked down at his EVA boots; they were covered with similar glittery splotches.

"A molecular osmotic is what they call it," Farrington continued. "It goes through anything, it goes right through your suit on contact by squeezing through the space between the molecules but won't cause your suit to lose its pressure. It invades living cells and inorganic molecules as well. Hell, it even goes through the hull—"

Then Farrington pointed to the floor, where thin, crisscrossing lines of the wet glitter shined.

Wentz was appalled. "They sent me up here *knowing* I'd get infected!"

"Yeah. But this stuff could kill everyone on Earth. What choice did they have?"

"No, what *right* did they have to send me to my death?" Wentz shouted.

Farrington frowned. "Put a lid on it, will you? Every time we climb into a cockpit we know we could die. It's part of the job. Hell, I'd have destroyed the probe myself but the EVA suits only have a hundred and twenty minutes of life-support. By the time their analysis determined that the shit up here was a deadly virus, my EVA gear was out of air. I couldn't make any more debarkations. I was trapped inside this tin can."

Wentz struggled to let the information sift in between his outrage.

"The QSR4 collector *had* to be destroyed. I no longer had the ability to unass this fuckin' crate and do it myself, so they determined that you were the best bet to get the second OEV up here successfully."

"Those lying sons of bitches!" Wentz railed.

"Give it a rest, man. We've flown in wars, we've flown in planes that no one else in the *world* has the rocks to fly. Risk is part of our duty. You knew that the minute you made your first test flight. So quit bellyaching. Quit acting like a little kid and start acting like what you are."

Wentz scowled. "What's that? A chump? What else am I but an Air Force sucker?"

"You're the best in the business," Farrington said. "You're the best to ever fly—you're even better than me."

Wentz just looked at him. Was there a tear in Farrington's eye?

"*You* are Operator 'A' now," Farrington said.

Wentz stood forlorn, eyes in a daze. Eventually the reality cracked him in the face. "How long...have I got?"

"I don't know. I've been here close to two months and I'm fading. Heartbeat's fucking up, dizzy spells, fever. Give yourself three months max."

Wentz gulped, nodded.

"Jill's with you, right?"

"Yeah."

"She tell you she's dying?"

"Yeah," Wentz said.

"She can handle this... But can you?"

"I think so," Wentz felt strong enough to say.

"Don't think about your family," Farrington added. "That just makes it worse. You'll want to kill yourself, which is what I almost did. Just think of it this way: you did it for them."

Wentz continued nodding. "Come with us," he offered. "I'll go back to my ship, get the second EVA suit, and bring it to you."

"Naw, I'm a loner, you know? Always have been. I've got more specs to pipe back to Earth. The apogee's only optimal seventeen minutes a day. And they pipe back ESPN for me, gives me a chance to catch the ball scores."

Wentz smiled. "Yankees man?"

"*Hell* no. Orioles. The only team that matters."

"Marines, what can I say? They're *all* fucked up."

Farrington laughed. "Hey, and tell Jill I said hi."

"I will..."

Farrington swung his feet off the bunk, coughed hard, then began to get up—

"Don't, sir," Wentz said.

"Fuck it." Farrington, after considerable effort, stood up straight. "At least you're not Navy. But I always knew there was some punk out there who was a better pilot than me."

"Sir, I'm not better than you by any stretch of the imagination."

Farrington grinned. "Yeah. Maybe you're right. Guess we'll never really know, will we?"

"Guess not, sir."

Farrington saluted; Wentz saluted back. Then Farrington extended his surgically- altered three-fingered right hand. Wentz awkwardly shook it with his own gloved hand.

"It's been an honor to meet you," Wentz said.

"Get the hell out of here," Farrington said. "And blow that piece of shit probe right the fuck up."

"With pleasure."

Wentz put his helmet back on, recharged his pressure, then entered the air-lock to exit the craft.

He set the pyrotechnic timer—the last thing to do—then trod back to his OEV. He took one long last gaze at the planet's desolate surface, then turned just in time to see the QRS4 collector explode spectacularly in dead silence. Brass-colored dust erupted, a twisted mushroom cloud in the near-vacuum conditions and, via the explosive's design, the debris shot upward in a straight plume.

So much for that, Wentz thought.

When the dust cleared, nothing at all remained.

CHAPTER 13

The pressure ducts hissed as the air-clock emptied. The interior hatch popped and Wentz stepped out. Ashton leaned sullenly against the commo chair.

"Is he still alive?"

"Yeah. He sends his regards."

Wentz labored to get out of the EVA gear. He threw it all into the corner.

And looked at Ashton.

"What now?" she asked. "Put me into the air-lock and eject me into space?"

"You should've told me."

"I wanted to once we were underway…but I had orders not to."

"Yeah, well you still should've told me, that's all."

"They were afraid you might bolt, abandon the mission and fly back to Earth."

Wentz's hands clenched into strange fists. He seethed. "I've never *abandoned* a mission in my life, and those sons of bitches know it."

"They couldn't take the chance," Ashton countered. "You know what's at stake here."

"Yeah…"

"And what could I do?" Ashton was growing irate. "Christ, I'm dying. I offered to do it. I offered to have the surgery and take the training, but it wouldn't have worked! It takes a *pilot's* mind, Jack. A *pilot's* reactions and a *pilot's* instincts. I couldn't have flown this thing in a million years."

Wentz slumped into the operator's seat. "I know. I'm just pissed off. I put up with the bullshit for twenty-five years...and now they give me one more mouthful."

"I'm eating from the same bowl, remember?" Ashton sat disgruntled in her own seat. "We had our jobs to do and we did them. We're in the military; sometimes we have to sacrifice ourselves. Others have—now it's our turn. And look at the payoff. Now the virus will never get to Earth."

Wentz errantly stroked his chin. "You're right, of course. It's a kick in the ass: women are always right."

"I won't disagree with you there." Ashton rolled up her sleeves. "I guess you've noticed—"

Wentz looked over. *Shit. The stuff moves fast.* The tiniest specks of the virus already could be seen on her arms. Then Wentz checked his own arms and noticed the same. On the OEV's deck, the faintest glittering traces had formed.

"Farrington said we've got three months if we're lucky," Wentz recounted.

"That's probably pretty accurate. The virus has an extended incubation period, which means infectees are contagious for a long time. That's why it's particularly dangerous."

But Wentz wasn't listening. The remaining realization was fully sinking in. "So we can't ever go back."

"No, Jack. Even if they quarantined us, the virus also attacks inorganic material, and it's osmotic—it goes through anything."

Wentz stared at the silence in the air as if it were a distant cloud. Everything he'd ever been seemed just as far away.

"The apogee's on," Ashton told him. "We've got video. Do you want to talk to them?"

Wentz sighed. "Why not?"

Ashton tapped a few keys on an auxiliary panel, flipped down a small liquid-plasma display screen. First there was only white fuzz and static, but then a grainy picture formed: General Rainier's face.

"Sorry about this, Wentz," his voice crackled. "But surely you realize—"

"I know," Wentz confessed.

"Did you destroy the collector probe?"

"Yes sir. It's space junk now."

"Good. You've made the ultimate sacrifice, Wentz. What you've done for your country and for the world is beyond—"

"Save it, General. But do me a favor, will you? I know you have to tell my wife and kid that I died in a test crash. But tell them I loved them, will you?"

"I will, Wentz. Personally."

Waves of static rose and fell.

"Is there anything else?"

"No, sir. I guess not," Wentz replied.

On the screen, now, Rainier was saluting. Then the screen fizzed and faded as contact was lost. Ashton turned off the display.

"I don't know about you but I could use a drink," Ashton commented.

Wentz scowled at her. "The bars close early up here."

But then Ashton whipped out a bottle of whiskey. "I smuggled this on in my flight pack. It's not Johnny Black but—"

Wentz grinned. "It'll work." He opened the bottle, took a swig, then passed it back. "So what do we do now? We can't go back to Earth."

"No, but look what we've got. We've got rations that will last months," Ashton reminded, "and a fuel-cell that'll produce all the water we need. And what else have we got?"

Wentz saw her point. "We've got an unlimited air supply and an unlimited fuel supply, not to mention a fully operational extraterrestrial vehicle capable of exceeding the speed of light."

"Um-hmm."

Wentz clapped his deformed hands together.

"Looks like we're going on the road trip of all time," he said.

"Go for it."

Wentz could feel the gleam in his eyes. The internal systems powered up when he pressed his hands into the detents. "Ready for take-off, Colonel?"

"Yes, sir."

The OEV began to hover upward.

"Now let's see what this alien spam can'll do…"

The craft rose a few more yards then shot away, heading for the universe.

ABOUT THE AUTHOR

Lee is the author of over 50 horror, fantasy, and sci-fi novels, and dozens of short stories. He has also had comic scripts published by DC Comics, Verotik Inc., and Cemetery Dance. Many of his novels have been reprinted in Germany, Poland, Japan, Italy, Romania, Greece, Russia, Spain and other countries. He is a Bram Stoker Award Nominee; his Lovecraftian novel INNSWICH HORROR won the 2010 Vincent Price Award for Best Foreign Book (Austria), his novel WHITE TRASH GOTHIC won the 2018 Splatterpunk Award for Best Extreme Horror Novel, and his collaborative novella HEADER 3 (with Ryan Harding) won for Best Extreme Novella. In 2020 Lee won the J.F. Gonzales Lifetime Achievement Award. In 2009, the movie version of his novella HEADER was released by Synapse Films; several of his novels are currently under option. Lee is a U.S. Army veteran and lives in Seminole, Florida.

Curious about other Crossroad Press books? Stop by our
website: http://crossroadpress.com
We offer quality writing
in digital, audio, and print formats.

Subscribe to our newsletter on the website homepage and
receive a free eBook.

www.ingramcontent.com/pod-product-compliance
Lightning Source LLC
Chambersburg PA
CBHW022030170626
46808CB00003B/1125